REX STOUT, the creator of Nero Wolfe, was born in Nobles-ville, Indiana, in 1886, the sixth of nine children of John and Lucetta Todhunter Stout, both Quakers. Shortly after his birth the family moved to Wakarusa, Kansas. He was edu-cated in a country school, but by the age of nine he was recognized throughout the state as a prodigy in arithmetic. Mr. Stout briefly attended the University of Kansas, but he left to enlist in the Navy and spent the next two years as a warrant officer on board President Theodore Roosevelt's yacht. When he left the Navy in 1908, Rex Stout began to write free-lance articles and worked as a sightseeing guide and an itinerant bookkeeper. Later he devised and imple-mented a school banking system which was installed in four hundred cities and towns throughout the country. In 1927 Mr. Stout retired from the world of finance and, with the proceeds of his banking scheme, left for Paris to write seri-ous fiction. He wrote three novels that received favorable reviews before turning to detective fiction. His first Nero Wolfe novel, *Fer-de-Lance*, appeared in 1934. It was followed by many others, among them, *Too Many Cooks*, *The Silent Speaker*, *If Death Ever Slept*, *The Doorbell Rang*, and *Please Pass the Guilt*, which established Nero Wolfe as a leading character on a par with Erle Stanley Gardner's famous pro-tagonist, Perry Mason. During World War II, Rex Stout waged a personal campaign against Nazism as chairman of the War Writers' Board, master of ceremonies of the radio program "Speaking of Liberty," and member of several national com-mittees. After the war he turned his attention to mobilizing public opinion against the wartime use of thermonuclear de-vices, was an active leader in the Authors' Guild, and re-sumed writing his Nero Wolfe novels. Rex Stout died in 1975 at the age of eighty-nine. A month before his death he pub-lished his seventy-second Nero Wolfe mystery, *A Family Af-fair*. Ten years later, a seventy-third Nero Wolfe mystery was discovered and published in *Death Times Three*.

The Rex Stout Library

*Available from Bantam Books

REX STOUT

Three Doors to Death

Introduction
by Jonathan Kellerman

BANTAM BOOKS
NEW YORK · TORONTO · LONDON · SYDNEY · AUCKLAND

A NERO WOLFE MYSTERY

THREE DOORS TO DEATH

A Bantam Crime Line Book / published by arrangement
with Viking Penguin

PUBLISHING HISTORY

Viking edition published January 1950
Mystery Guild edition published 1950
Included in Viking edition of *Five of a Kind*,
The Third Nero Wolfe Omnibus published 1961
Bantam edition / June 1966
New Bantam edition / May 1970
Bantam reissue edition / March 1995

Acknowledgment is made to THE AMERICAN MAGAZINE, in which these three
short novels originally appeared: "Man Alive," December 1947; "Omit
Flowers," November 1948; and "Door to Death," June 1949.

CRIME LINE and the portrayal of a boxed "cl" are trademarks of Bantam
Books, a division of Random House, Inc.

ISBN 978-0-553-25127-2
Published simultaneously in the United States and Canada

Bantam Books are published by Bantam Books, a division of Random House,
Inc. Its trademark, consisting of the words "Bantam Books" and the portrayal
of a rooster, is Registered in U.S. Patent and Trademark Office and in other
countries. Marca Registrada. Bantam Books, 1540 Broadway, New York, New
York 10036.

PRINTED IN THE UNITED STATES OF AMERICA

Introduction

L et's face it.

We can stare at each other over designer coffee and natter on about the spiritual and intellectual benefits of immersing oneself in *haute littérature*, but most of us read fiction to get away from the drudgery of our lives.

And what a wonderful sanctuary Rex Stout has provided millions of readers for over half a century by introducing the world to Nero Wolfe.

As the century fades, Wolfe lives on, fresh and current as ever. One reason is the *way* he lives—a self-contained, blatantly self-indulgent existence in a Manhattan brownstone on West Thirty-fifth Street surrounded by gleaming paneling, fine furniture, gourmet food, servants, exotic orchids, the power to control life's nasty little intrusions. What a glorious end-of-day tonic for clock watchers, straphangers, and freeway slaves. How many of us wouldn't commit minor mayhem in exchange for an Archie Goodwin to cheerfully run our errands and tidy up our scutwork, or a Fritz Brenner to prepare and serve our sweetbreads en croûte on bone china? With a suitable wine. (Interestingly, Wolfe's cozy world also burlesques the isolated, self-indulgent life of the writer and, in that sense, can be regarded as Stout's wicked slant on the *artiste*.)

Stout had wicked slants on lots of things and a gift for phrasing and rhythm and irony that remains remarkably contemporary. Consider lines such as these: "Her chin hinges began to give"; "the sort of greasy voice that makes me want to take up strangling"; "he was slender, elegant, and groomed to a queen's taste, if you let him pick the queen." And let us not forget the hilariously truistic: "Escorting a murderer on a subway without handcuffs is a damn nuisance, so I chose a taxi."

Stout's sense of humor is at its best when it conveys a lusty misanthropy. Wolfe's truculent view of his fellow men—and women—is delicious in an age when sectarian selfishness and emotional lobotomy masquerade as political correctness and the carny freak parade is beamed into our homes daily in the form of pretentiously mislabeled *talk* shows so self-righteously smarmy they gag the consciousness. Take a blissful moment to imagine Wolfe on *Geraldo* or *Oprah* or any of the other high-octane patholothons. I, for one, would commit *major* mayhem for the privilege of witnessing it. Hell, one good "Pfui!" directed at a celibopsychic schizoid diaper devotee would be worth it.

Then there's Wolfe's glorious gluttony, a perfect foil for the skeletal images and anorexic fiction promulgated with teeth-gnashing joy by the style-over-substance crowd. Stout doesn't spare Wolfe the consequences of his hyperphagia—the Great Man is so monstrously endomorphic that when he removes his pajama top, he reveals "enough hide to make shoes for four platoons;" but he does not assault us with cholesterol counts and dire warnings of vascular sludge. During the time we spend gourmandizing along with Wolfe, the nagging and finger-wagging of gram-counting aerobicops fade mercifully into the background. Wolfe may huff and puff during his infrequent outings into the "real" world—the description of his unplanned hike in the final story in this volume is as memorable as anything that has ever been put to paper—but he is happy with himself. And when we are with him, so are we, by God.

Of course there's more to Wolfe than constructive agoraphobia or cream sauce. Stout's stories are always great mysteries—whodunits, howdunits, whydunits—and they zip along at a pace that would leave the Great Man anoxic.

Some say Stout's talents were put to best use in the novella, and no contradiction of that judgment can be found in the three stories in this book.

Turn the page, then, and prepare yourself for a well-deserved getaway: the funny, phony, bloody world of high fashion as portrayed in "Man Alive." The knife-in-the-back shenanigans of the nascent fast-food industry in "Omit Flowers" (how sadly civilized that bit of vulgarity seems compared to today's technoburger madness). And finally, the spooky and downright nasty family psychopathology of "Door to Death," a real chiller.

Three gems.

Three great escapes.

—Jonathan Kellerman

Contents

Foreword

Looking over the scripts of these accounts of three of Nero Wolfe's cases, it struck me that they might give a stranger a wrong impression of him, so I thought it wouldn't hurt to put in this foreword for those who haven't met him before. In only one of these cases did he get paid—I mean paid money—for working on it, and that might give someone a woolly idea which could develop into a nuisance. I want to make it clear that Wolfe does not solve murders just for the hell of it. He does it to make a living, which includes me, since he can't live the way he likes to without signing my pay check each and every Friday afternoon. Also please note that in the other two cases he did get something: in one, the satisfaction of doing a favor for an old and dear friend, and in the other, a fill-in for Theodore.

With that warning, I like the idea of putting these three cases together because they make a kind of complicated pattern of pairs. In two of them Wolfe got no fee. In two of them he had to forget a document to get a crack started. In two of them the homicide was strictly a family affair. In two of them I became acquainted with a young female, not the same one, who might have sent my pulse up a beat if she hadn't been quite so close to a murder. So I think they'll be a little more interesting, in a bunch like this, provided they don't start people phoning in to ask me to ask Wolfe to solve murders as a gift. I'm just telling you.

Archie Goodwin

Three Doors
to Death

Man Alive

I

She said, in her nicely managed voice that was a pleasure to listen to, "Daumery and Nieder."

I asked her politely, "Will you spell it, please?"

I meant the Daumery, since I already had the
Nieder down in my notebook, her name being, so she
had said, Cynthia Nieder.

Her lovely bright blue eyes changed expression to
show that she suspected me of kidding her—as if I
had asked her to spell Shakespeare or Charlie Chap-
lin. But I was so obviously innocent that the eyes
changed again and she smiled.

She spelled Daumery and added, "Four ninety-six
Seventh Avenue. That's what we get for being so
cocky about how famous we are—we get asked how to
spell it. What if someone asked you how to spell Nero
Wolfe?"

"Try it," I suggested, smiling back at her. I extended a hand. "Put your fingers on my pulse and ask
me. But don't ask me how to spell Archie Goodwin,
which is me. That would hurt."

Wolfe grunted peevishly and readjusted a few

hundred of his pounds in his built-to-order high-test chair behind his desk. "You made," he told our visitor, "an appointment to see me. I supposed you needed a detective. If so tell me what for, without encouraging Mr. Goodwin to start caterwauling. It takes very little to set him off."

I let it go by, though I am much more particular than his insult implied. I felt like indulging him because he had just bought a new Cadillac sedan, which meant that I, Archie Goodwin, had a new car, because, of the four men who lived in Nero Wolfe's brownstone house on West 35th Street not far from the river, I was the only one who drove. Wolfe himself, who suspected all machinery with moving parts of being in a plot to get him, rarely left the house for any reason whatever, and never—well, hardly ever— on business. He stayed in his office, on the ground floor of the house, and used his brain if and when I could pester him into it. Fritz Brenner, chef and supervisor of household comforts, knew how to drive but pretended he didn't, and had no license. Theodore Horstmann, curator of the orchids in the plant rooms on the roof, thought walking was good for people and was still, at his age, trying to prove it.

That left me. In addition to being chief assistant detective, bookkeeper and stenographer, the flea in the elephant's ear, and balance wheel, I was also chauffeur and errand boy. Therefore the new car was, in effect, mine, and I thought I ought to show my appreciation by letting him call me a tomcat at least once. Another thing, the car had cost plenty, and we hadn't been offered an acceptable job for over a week. We could use a fee. The blue-eyed female treat looked as if she wasn't short on cash, and if I riled Wolfe about a little thing like a personal insult he might react by broadening out and insulting her too, and she might go somewhere else to shop.

So all I did was grin understandingly at Cynthia Nieder, brandish my pen over my notebook, and clear my throat.

II

"Daumery and Nieder," Cynthia said, "is as good a name as there is on Seventh Avenue, including Fifty-seventh Street, but of course if you're not in the garment trade and know nothing about it—I imagine your wives would know the name all right."

Wolfe shuddered.

"No wife," I stated. "Neither of us. That's why we caterwaul."

"Well, if you had one she would know about Daumery and Nieder. We make top-quality coats, suits, and dresses, and we confine our line, even here in New York. The business was started twenty years ago by two men, Jean Daumery and Paul Nieder—my Uncle Paul—my father's brother. It's—"

"Excuse me," Wolfe put in. "Will it save time to tell you that I don't do industrial surveillance?"

"No, that's not it," she said, waving it away. "I know you don't. It's about him, my uncle. Uncle Paul."

She frowned, and was looking at the window beyond Wolfe's desk as if she were seeing something. Then her shoulders lifted and dropped again, and she went back to Wolfe.

"You need some background," she told him. "At least I think it would be better. Daumery was the business head of the firm, the organizer and manager and salesman, and Uncle Paul was the designer, the creator. If it hadn't been for him Daumery wouldn't have had anything to manage and sell. They owned it together—a fifty-fifty partnership. It was my uncle's half that I inherited when my uncle killed himself—anyway, that's how it was announced, that he committed suicide—a little over a year ago."

That gave me two thoughts: one, that I had been right about her having the price of a fee; and two, that we were probably in for another job of translating a suicide into a murder.

"I suppose I should tell about me," Cynthia was saying. "I was born and brought up out West, in Oregon. My father and mother died when I was fourteen, and Uncle Paul sent for me, and I came to New York and lived with him. He wasn't married. We didn't get along very well together, I guess because we were so much alike, because I'm creative too; but it wasn't really so bad, we just fought all the time. And when it came down to it he let me have my way. He was determined about my going to college, but I knew I was creative and it would be a waste of time. We fought about it every day, and finally he said if I didn't go to college I would have to earn my living, and then what do you think he did? He gave me a job modeling for Daumery and Nieder at top salary! That's what he was like! Actually he was wonderful. He gave me the run of the place too, to catch on about designing, but of course he wouldn't have done that if he hadn't known I had unusual talent."

"What kind of talent?" Wolfe asked skeptically.

"As a clothes designer, of course," she said, as if that were the only talent worth mentioning. "I was only eighteen—that was three years ago—and completely without training, and for two years I only modeled and caught onto things, but I had a few little chances to show what I could do. I was surprised that my uncle was willing to help me along, because most established designers are so jealous; but he did. Then he went West on a vacation, and then the word came that he had killed himself. Maybe I ought to tell you why I wasn't surprised that he had killed himself."

"Maybe," Wolfe conceded.

"Because I knew how unhappy he was. Helen Daumery had died. A horse she was riding had gone crazy and thrown her off on some stones and killed her. She was Daumery's wife—the wife of my uncle's partner—and my uncle was in love with her. She had been one of their models—she was much younger than Daumery—and I think she was the only woman Uncle Paul ever loved—anyhow he certainly loved her. She didn't love him because she didn't love anybody but herself, but I think she probably gave him the cherry out of her cocktail just because she enjoyed having him like that when no other woman could get him. She would."

I didn't put it in my notes that Miss Nieder had disapproved of Mrs. Daumery, but I could have, and signed it.

"Helen's death broke my uncle up completely," Cynthia went on. "I never saw anything like it. I was still living in his apartment. He didn't say a word to me for three days—not a single word—nor to anyone else, and he didn't leave the apartment day or night— right in the middle of getting ready for the showings of the fall line—and then he said he was going away for a rest, and he went. Four days later the news came that he had committed suicide, and under the circumstances it didn't occur to me to question it."

When she paused Wolfe inquired, "Do you question it now?"

"I certainly do," she said emphatically. "I wasn't surprised, either, at the way he did it. He was always keyed up and dramatic, about everything. He was by far the best designer in New York, and he was the best showman, too. So you would expect him to do something startling about killing himself, no matter how unhappy he was. He took all his clothes off and jumped into a geyser in Yellowstone Park."

Wolfe let out a mild grunt. I gave her an admiring eye for her calm voice and manner in dishing out a fact like that, but of course it was a year old for her.

"Under the surface of that geyser," she said, "down below, the pressure in the pipe from above keeps the temperature far above the boiling point, according to an article about it I read in a newspaper."

"That seems conclusive," Wolfe murmured. "Why do you now question it?"

"Because he didn't die. Because he's not dead. I saw him last week, here in New York, alive."

III

I felt myself relaxing. It had seemed that we were about to be tagged for the chore of ripping the false face off of a murder disguised as a suicide, and at the smell of murder I always go tight all over. In the detective business that's the center ring in the big tent. The headline MAN DEAD gets the eye good, but Cynthia Nieder had scrapped that and changed it to MAN ALIVE, which was quite a comedown. Another thought had struck me: that if Uncle Paul was alive her inheriting half the business was out the window and her ability to pay a good exorbitant fee was open to question. My attitude toward her personally remained intact; she rated high priority on looks, voice, and other observable factors. But professionally I was compelled to grade her way down in the little routine items.

So I relaxed and tossed my notebook on my desk, which is so placed that a half-turn of my swivel chair puts me facing Wolfe, and with another half-turn I am confronting the red leather chair beyond the end of his desk where a lone visitor is usually seated. Some visitors clash with it, but Cynthia, in a deep-toned yellow dress, maybe silk, a jacket in brown and yellow checks, flaring open, and a little brown affair slanting on her head, looked fine. Having learned one or two little things about women's clothes from Lily Rowan and other reliable sources, I decided that if Cynthia had designed that outfit Wolfe should eat his skepticism about her talent.

She was talking, telling about the man alive.

"It was last Tuesday," she said, "a week ago tomorrow, June third. We were showing our fall line to the press. We don't show in hotels because we don't have to, since our showroom seats over two hundred comfortably. For a press showing we don't let anyone in without a ticket because if we did the place would be mobbed. I was modeling a blue and black ensemble of lightweight Bishop twill when I saw him. He was in the fifth row, between Agnes Pemberton of *Vogue* and Mrs. Gumpert of the *Herald Tribune*. If you asked me how I recognized him I couldn't tell you, but I simply knew it was him, there wasn't the slightest doubt—"

"Why shouldn't you recognize him?" Wolfe demanded.

"Because he had a beard, and he wore glasses, and his hair was slick and parted on the left side. That sounds like a freak, but Uncle Paul would know better than to look freaky. The beard was trimmed, and somehow it didn't make him conspicuous. It was lucky I didn't completely recognize him when I first saw him, or I would probably have stood and gawked at him. Later in the dressing room Polly Zarella asked Bernard—that's Bernard Daumery, Jean's nephew— who was the man that was growing his own wool, and Bernard said he didn't know, probably from the *Daily Worker*. Of course we know most of the guests at a press showing, but not all of them. When I modeled another number—a full-back calf-covering coat in tapestry tones of Kleinsell ratiné—I took him in without being obvious about it, and all of a sudden I knew who it was—I didn't guess, I *knew*. It staggered me so that I had to get off quick, quicker than I should have, and in the dressing room it was all I could do to keep them from seeing me tremble. I wanted to run out and speak to him, but I couldn't because it would have ruined the show. I had four more numbers to model— one of them was our headliner, a tailored dress and jacket in black with white stripes, with slightly bouffant sleeves and a double hemline—and I had to go on to the end. When it was over I hurried out front and he was gone."

"Indeed," Wolfe muttered.

"Yes. I went outside, to the elevators, but he was gone."

"You haven't seen him since?"

"No. Just that one time."

"Did anyone else recognize him?"

"I don't think so. I'm sure they didn't, or there would have been a noise. A dead man come back to life?"

Wolfe nodded. "Many of those present had known him?"

"Certainly, nearly all of them. He was famous, as famous as you are."

Wolfe skipped that one. "How sure are you it was he?"

"I'm absolutely positive. There simply isn't any argument about it."

"Did you find out who he was supposed to be?"

She shook her head. "I couldn't find out a thing about him. I didn't want to ask questions of too many people, but no one could tell me anything." She hesitated. "I must admit the ticket thing is handled pretty loosely. The tickets aren't just scattered around, but anyone who knows the ropes wouldn't have much trouble getting one, and my uncle certainly knows the ropes."

"Whom have you told about this?"

"No one. Not a soul. I've been trying to decide what to do."

"You might," Wolfe suggested, "just erase it. You say you inherited a half-interest in that"—he grimaced—"that business from your uncle?"

"Yes."

"Anything else? Property, securities, money in the bank?"

"No. He had no property, except the furniture in his apartment, and the lawyer said there were no securities or bank accounts."

"Hunh," Wolfe said. "Those are portable. But you have half of that business. Is it solvent?"

Cynthia smiled. "As Polly Zarella puts it, we grossed over two million last year with a swelled-up profit."

"Then why not erase it, if your uncle likes his beard and his hair slicked? If you corner him and make him shave and wash his hair, and make him take his old label, you'll have no share of the swelled-up profits. He will. I would charge moderately for this interview."

"No." She shook her head emphatically. "I have to know what's going on, and I have to know where I stand. I—" She stopped and bit her lip. Apparently she had been keeping emotions, whatever they might be, under control, and they were trying to break loose. When she was ready for speech again all she said was, "I'm upset."

"Then you should reserve decision." Wolfe was being very patient with her. "Never decide anything while you're upset." He wiggled a finger. "And in spite of your dogmatism you may be wrong. True, you might have recognized him when others didn't, since you lived with him and knew him intimately, but others knew him intimately too. One especially—his business partner, Mr. Daumery—for twenty years, you say. Was he there that day and did he see the man with the beard?"

Cynthia's eyes had widened. "Oh," she exclaimed, "didn't I—I thought I had mentioned that! Of course Bernard Daumery, the nephew, was there—I know I mentioned him—but Jean Daumery, my uncle's partner, he's dead!"

Wolfe's eyes opened to more than a slit for the first time. "The devil he is. Jumped in a geyser?"

"No, in an accident. He was drowned. He was fishing and fell from the boat."

"Where was this?"

"In Florida. Off the west coast."

"When?"

"It was—let's see, today is June ninth—a little over six weeks ago."

"Who was on the boat with him?"

"Bernard, his nephew."

"Anyone else?"

"No."

"And the nephew inherited that half?"

"Yes, but—" She frowned. Her hand fluttered. She had a habit of making gestures which were graceful and a pleasure to look at. "But that's all right."

"Why is it all right?"

"That's a silly question," she said with spirit. "I merely mean that if there had been any question of anything wrong the Florida people would have attended to it."

"Perhaps," Wolfe conceded grumpily. "Only it's quite a list. Mrs. Daumery thrown from a horse onto stones and killed. Mr. Nieder propelled into a geyser and boiled. Mr. Daumery hurtled into an ocean and drowned. It's not my affair, thank heaven, but if it were I should want better testimony than that of what you call the Florida people." He got brusque. "About your uncle, what do you want me for?"

She knew the answer to that one. "I want you to find him, and I want to see him."

"Very well. It may take time and it will be expensive. A retainer of two thousand dollars?"

She didn't blink. "Of course," she agreed, speaking as a millionaire. "I'll mail you a check today. I suppose it's understood that this is extremely confidential, as I said at the beginning, and no reports are to be phoned to me, and written reports are not to be mailed but handed to me personally. One thing I was going to suggest."

She directed her clear blue eyes at me, and back at Wolfe.

"I'll be glad," she said, "to tell you all I know about his former associates, but I doubt if that will help. He had no relatives but me, and no really close friends that I know of. The only person he ever loved was Helen Daumery—unless he had some affection for me; I guess maybe he did. But he loved designing, his work, and he loved that business. I think he came there last Tuesday because he simply couldn't stay away. I don't believe he knew I recognized him, so why wouldn't he come back? If he does, it will probably be today, because this afternoon we have our big show of the fall line for buyers. That's why I came to see you this morning. He wouldn't even need a ticket, and I have a feeling he'll be there. I know you do everything in your office and practically never go out, but couldn't Mr. Goodwin come? He could sit near the front, and I could arrange to give him a signal if I see my uncle—only he would have to be extremely careful not to spoil the show in any way—"

Wolfe was nodding at her. "Excellent," he declared.

IV

At 2:55 that Monday afternoon in June I entered the building at 496 Seventh Avenue and took an elevator to the twelfth floor.

Since that was only a ten-minute walk from Wolfe's place my choice would have been to hoof it, but Wolfe was proceeding to spend chunks of the two grand even before he got it. He had called in Saul Panzer, the best free-lance operative on earth, and Saul and I went together in a taxi driven by our old pal Herb Aronson, whom we often used. Saul and Herb stayed at the curb in the cab, with the flag down. It had developed that Cynthia didn't want Uncle Paul's whiskers yanked off in any public spot, and therefore he would have to be tailed. Tailing in New York, if you really mean it, being no one-man job, we were setting it up right, with me on foot and Saul on wheels.

Cynthia had filled in a few gaps before leaving our office. She had inherited her uncle's half of the business under a will he had left, but was not yet in legal possession because of the law's attitude about dead people who leave no remains. There had been no serious doubt of his being pressure-cooked in the geyser, though no one had actually seen him jump in, since his clothes had been found at the geyser's rim, and the farewell letters in the pocket of the coat, one to his lawyer and one to his niece, had unquestionably been in his handwriting. But the law was chewing its cud. Apparently Jean Daumery, up to the moment he had fallen off the boat and got drowned, had done likewise, and, in the six weeks since his death, his nephew Bernard had carried on with the chewing. That was the impression I got from a couple of Cynthia's remarks about her current status at Daumery and Nieder's. She was still modeling, and most of the designing was being done by a guy named Ward Roper, whose name she pronounced with a good imitation of the inflection Winston Churchill used in pronouncing Mussolini.

She had got in another dig or two at Helen Daumery, replying to Wolfe's casual questions. It was possible, she said, that Jean Daumery had known what was going on between his wife and his business partner, but it was doubtful because Helen had been an extremely slick article. And when Wolfe inquired about Helen's death and Cynthia told him that it happened on a country lane where Helen and her husband were out for a Sunday morning ride on their own horses, and the husband was the only eyewitness, she added that whoever or whatever was in charge of accidents might as well get the credit for that one, and that anyway Jean Daumery was dead too.

So it still looked as if we were fresh out of murders as far as Cynthia was concerned. To get any attention from Wolfe a murder must be attached to a client with money to spend and a reason for spending it. Cynthia didn't fit. As for her uncle, he wasn't dead. As for Helen Daumery, Cynthia wasn't interested a nickel's worth. As for Jean Daumery, Cynthia was stringing along with the Florida people who had decided there was nothing wrong.

Therefore there was no tingle in me as I got off the elevator at the twelfth floor.

Double doors were standing open, with a few human beings gathered there. As I approached, a bulky female who had been in my elevator swept past me and was going on through, but a man sidestepped to cut her off and asked politely, "What is your firm, please?"

The woman glared at him. "Coats and suits for Driscoll's Emporium, Tulsa."

The man shook his head. "Sorry, there's no place for you." His face suddenly lit up with a cordial smile, and I thought unexpected grace was about to drop on her until I saw that the smile was for another one from my elevator, a skinny dame with big ears.

"Good after*noon*, Miss Dixon," the smiler said, serving it with sugar. "Mr. Roper was asking about you just a minute ago."

Miss Dixon nodded indifferently and went on in. I maneuvered around Driscoll's Emporium, who was looking enraged but impotent, and murmured at the man in a refined voice.

"My name is Goodwin, British Fabrics Association. Miss Cynthia Nieder invited me. Shall I wait while you check with her?"

He looked me over and I took it without flinching, wearing, as I was, a tropical worsted tailored by Breslow and a shirt and tie that were fully worthy. "It isn't necessary," he finally conceded and motioned me through.

The room was so nearly packed that it took a couple of minutes to find an empty seat far enough front to be sure of catching Cynthia's signal, which was to be brushing her hair back on the right side with her left hand. I saw no point in pretending I wasn't there, and before sitting down I turned in a slow complete circle, giving the audience the eye as if I were looking for a friend. There were close to two hundred of them, and I was surprised to see that nearly a third of them were men, though Cynthia had explained that they would be not only buyers from all over the country, but also merchandise executives, department heads, presidents, vice-presidents, fashion writers, fabrics people, and miscellaneous.

I saw no one with whiskers.

Also before sitting I picked up, from the chair, a pad of paper and a pencil. The pad consisted of sheets with DAUMERY AND NIEDER and the address neatly printed in an upper corner. I was supposed, as I soon learned from watching my neighbors, to use it for making notes about the numbers I wanted to buy. On my right was a plump gray-haired specimen with sweat below her ear, and on my left was a handsome woman with an extremely good mouth, fairly young but not quite young enough. Neither had given me more than an indifferent glance.

The room was high-ceilinged, and the wood-paneled walls were pretty well covered with drawings and photographs. Aside from that, and us on our chairs, there was nothing but a large raised platform, in the open space between the front row of seats and the wall beyond. That wall had two doors, twenty feet apart. I had been seated only a minute or two when the door on the left opened and a woman emerged. She was old enough to be my mother but wasn't. My mother wouldn't use that much lipstick in a year, and her shoulders would never get that much padding no matter what high fashion said.

The woman stood a moment, looking us over, turned to signal to someone through the open door, closed the door, and went to a chair near the end of the front row that had evidently been held for her. She was no sooner seated than the door opened again and out came the girl that I was waiting to marry. I put my teeth together to keep from whistling. I got the impression that she was the girl they were all waiting to marry, seeing how concentrated and alert everyone became the second she appeared, and then I realized what this meant to the buyers. For them it was the make or break. It meant their jobs. They had just so many thousands to spend, on so many numbers, and it was up to them to pick the winners or else.

Anyone could have picked the girl with one eye shut, but they weren't picking girls. She stepped up on the platform, came to the front edge, walking in a highly trained manner, extended her arms to the sides, full out, and said in a clear and friendly voice, "Six-forty-two." Six-forty-two was a dress and coat, looking like wool and I suppose it was, sort of confused about colors like a maple tree in October. She gave it the works. She walked to the right and then to the left, threw her arms around to show that the seams would hold even if you got in a fight or wore it picking apples, and turned around to let us see the back. She said "Six-forty-two" four times altogether, at appropriate intervals, distinctly and amiably, with just the faintest suggestion in her voice and manner that she wouldn't dream of letting that out except to the few people she was very fond of; and when she took the coat off and draped it over her arm and lifted her chin to smile at the back row, there was some clapping of hands.

She left by the other door, the one on the right, and immediately the one on the left opened and out came the girl I was waiting to marry, only this was a blonde, and she had on a gray fur evening wrap lined in bright red, and what she said was "Three-eighty and Four-nineteen." The 380, I gathered from neighbors' mutterings, was the wrap, and the 419 was the simple red evening gown that was disclosed when she ditched the wrap. It was fairly simple in front at the top, just covering essentials, but at the back it got even simpler by simply not starting until it hit the waistline. The woman on my right whispered to the one on her other side, "The hell of that is I've got a customer that would love it but I wouldn't dare let her buy it."

To clear up one point, they had there that afternoon six of the girls I was waiting to marry, if you count Cynthia Nieder, and I don't see why you shouldn't. Each of them made around a dozen appearances, some more, some less, and as for picking and choosing, if the buyers were as far up a stump as I was by the time it was over the only way they could possibly handle it was to send in an order for one of each.

As I explained to Wolfe in the office that evening, after I had reported a blank and we were conversing, "Imagine it! After the weddings I will of course have to take a good-sized apartment between Fifth and Madison in the Sixties. On a pleasant autumn evening I'll be sitting in the living room reading the newspaper. I'll toss the paper aside and clap my hands, and in will come Isabel. She will have on a calf-exposing kitchen apron with a double hemline and will be carrying a plate of ham sandwiches and a pitcher of milk. She will say seductively, 'Two-ninety-three,' make interesting motions and gestures without spilling a drop, put the plate and pitcher on a table at my elbow, and go. In will come Francine. She will be wearing slim-silhouette pajamas with padded shoulders and a back-flaring hipline. She'll walk and wave and whirl, say 'Nine-thirty-one' four times, and light me a cigarette and dance out. Enter Delia. She'll be dressed in a high-styled bra of hand-made lace with a billowing sweep to the—"

"Pfui," Wolfe said curtly. "Enter another, naked, carrying a basket full of bills, your checkbook, and a pen."

He has a personal slant on women.

Back to the show. It lasted over two hours, and for some of the numbers the applause was unrestrained, and it looked to me as if the Daumery and Nieder profits were likely to go on swelling up. Cynthia, in my opinion, was the star, and others seemed to agree with me. The numbers she modeled got much more applause than the rest of the line, and I admit I furnished my share, which was as it should be since I was her guest. Remarks from my neighbor on the right, who was evidently in the know, informed me that Cynthia's numbers had all been designed by herself, whereas the others were the work of Ward Roper, who had been Paul Nieder's assistant and was merely a good imitator and adapter.

In the office that evening I explained that to Wolfe, too, partly because I knew it would bore and irritate him, and partly because I wanted to demonstrate that I hadn't been asleep although my report of results had had no bodice at all and a very short skirt.

A breath and a half had done it. "I got in by following Cynthia's instructions, found a seat in the fifth row, and sat down after doing a survey of the two hundred customers and seeing no whiskers. Miss Nieder made fourteen appearances and did not signal me. When she came out front after the show she was immediately encircled by people, and I beat it, again following instructions, went down to the sidewalk, told Saul nothing doing, and handed Herb Aronson a ten-dollar bill."

Wolfe grunted. "What next?"

"That requires thought, which is your department. We can't sick the cops on him because the client doesn't want that. We can buy a gross of combs and comb the city. Or we can try again at their next show for buyers, which, as you know, will be Thursday morning at ten. Or you may remember what the client said about her uncle's private file."

Wolfe poohed. "She doesn't even know whether it exists. She thinks Jean Daumery took it and locked it up, and that the nephew, Bernard Daumery, is hanging onto it. She thinks she may possibly be able to find it."

"Okay, you admit she thinks, so why not you? You're merely objecting, not thinking. Think."

That was before dinner. If he did put his brain in motion there were no visible or audible results. After dinner, back in the office again, he started reading a book. That disgusted me, because after all we had a case, and for the sake of appearances I started in on a blow-by-blow account of the Daumery and Nieder show. The least I could do was to make it hard for him to read. I went on for over an hour, covering the ground, and then branched out into commentary.

"Imagine it!" I said. "After the weddings I will of course have to take a good-sized apartment . . ."

I've already told about that.

The next morning, Tuesday, he was still shirking. When we have a job on he usually has breakfast instructions for me before he goes up to the plant rooms for his nine-to-eleven session with Theodore and the orchids, but that day there wasn't a peep out of him, and when he came down to the office at eleven o'clock he got himself comfortable in his chair behind his desk, rang for Fritz to bring beer—two short buzzes —and picked up his book. Even when I showed him the check from Cynthia which had come in the morning mail, two thousand smackers, he merely nodded indifferently. I snorted at him and strode to the hall and out the front door, on my way to the bank to make a deposit. When I got back he was on his second bottle of beer and deep in his book. Apparently his idea was to go on reading until Thursday's show for buyers.

For one o'clock lunch in the dining room, which was across the hall from the office, Fritz served us with chicken livers and tomato halves fried in oil and trimmed with chopped peppers and parsley, followed by rice cakes and honey. I took it easy on the livers because of my attitude toward Fritz's rice cakes. I was on my fifth cake, or maybe sixth, when the doorbell rang. During meals Fritz always answers the door, on account of Wolfe's feeling that the main objection to atom bombs is that they may interrupt people eating. Through the open door from the dining room to the hall I saw Fritz pass on his way to the front, and a moment later his voice came, trying to persuade someone to wait in the office until Wolfe had finished lunch. There was no other voice, but there were steps, and then our visitor was marching in on us—a man about Wolfe's age, heavy-set, muscular, red-faced, and obviously aggressive.

It was our chum Inspector Cramer, head of Homicide. He advanced to the table before he stopped and spoke to Wolfe.

"Hello. Sorry to break in on your meal."

"Good morning," Wolfe said courteously. For him it was always morning until he had finished his lunch coffee. "If you haven't had lunch we can offer you—"

"No, thanks, I'm busy and in a hurry. A woman named Cynthia Nieder came to see you yesterday."

Wolfe put a piece of rice cake in his mouth. I had a flash of a thought: Good God, the client's dead.

"Well?" Cramer demanded.

"Well what?" Wolfe snapped. "You stated a fact. I'm eating lunch."

"Fine. It's a fact. What did she want?"

"You know my habits and customs, Mr. Cramer."

Wolfe was controlling himself. "I never talk business at a meal. I invited you to join us and you declined. If you will wait in the office—"

Cramer slapped a palm on the table, rattling things. My guess was that Wolfe would throw the coffee pot, since it was the heaviest thing handy, but I couldn't stay for it because along with the sound of Cramer's slap the doorbell rang again, and I thought I'd better not leave this one to Fritz. I got up and went, and through the one-way glass panel in the front door I saw an object that relieved me. The client was still alive and apparently unhurt. She was standing there on the stoop.

I pulled the door open, put my finger on my lips, muttered at her, "Keep your mouth shut," and with one eye took in the police car parked at the curb, seven steps down from the stoop. The man seated behind the wheel, a squad dick with whom I was acquainted, was looking at us with an expression of interest. I waved at him, signaled Cynthia to enter, shut the door, and elbowed her into the front room, which faces the street and adjoins the office.

She looked scared, untended, haggard, and determined.

"The point is," I told her, "that a police inspector named Cramer is in the dining room asking about you. Do you want to see him?"

"Oh." She gazed at me as if she were trying to remember who I was. "I've already seen him." She looked around, saw a chair, got to it, and sat. "They've been—asking me—questions for hours—"

"Why, what happened?"

"My uncle—" Her head went forward and she covered her face with her hands. In a moment she looked up at me and said, "I want to see Nero Wolfe," and then covered her face with her hands again.

It might, I figured, take minutes to nurse her to the point of forming sentences. So I told her, "Stay here and sit tight. The walls are soundproofed, but keep quiet anyhow."

When I rejoined them in the dining room the coffee pot was still on the table unthrown, but the battle was on. Wolfe was out of his chair, erect, rigid with rage.

"No, sir," he was saying in his iciest tone, "I have not finished my gobbling now, as you put it. I would have eaten two more cakes, and I have not had my coffee. You broke in, and you're here. If you were not an officer of the law Mr. Goodwin would knock you unconscious and drag you out."

He moved. He stamped to the door, across the hall, and into the office. I was right behind him. By the time Cramer was there, seated in the red leather chair, Wolfe was seated too, behind his desk, breathing at double speed, with his mouth closed tight.

"Forget it," Cramer rasped, trying to make up.

Wolfe was silent.

"All I want," Cramer said, "is to find out why Cynthia Nieder came to see you. You have a right to ask why I want to know, and I would have told you if you hadn't lost your temper just because I arrived while you were stuffing it in. There's been a murder."

Wolfe said nothing.

"Last night," Cramer went on. "Time limits, eight P.M. and midnight. At the place of business of Daumery and Nieder on the twelfth floor of Four-ninety-six Seventh Avenue. Cynthia Nieder was there last night between nine and nine-thirty, she admits that; and nobody else as far as we know now. She says she went to get some drawings, but that's got holes in it. The body was found this morning, lying in the middle of the floor in the office. He had been hit in the back of the head with a hardwood pole, one of those used to raise and lower windows, and the end of the pole with the brass hook on it had been jabbed into his face a dozen times or more—like spearing a fish."

Wolfe had his eyes closed. I was considering that after all Cramer was the head of Homicide and he was paid for handling murders, and he always tried hard and deserved a little encouragement, so I asked in a friendly manner, "Who was it?"

"Nobody knows," he said sarcastically and without returning the friendliness. "A complete stranger to all the world, and nothing on him to tell." He paused, and then suddenly barked at me, "*You* describe him!"

"Nuts. Who was it?"

"It was a medium-sized man around forty, with a brown beard and slick brown hair parted on the left side, with glasses that were just plain glass. Can you name him?"

I thought it extremely interesting that Cramer's description consisted of the three items that Cynthia had specified. It showed what a well-planned disguise could do.

V

Wolfe remained silent.

"Sorry," I said. "Never met him."

Cramer left me for Wolfe. "Under the circumstances," he argued, still sarcastic, "you may concede that I have a right to ask what she came to you for. It was only after she tried two lies on us about how she spent yesterday morning that we finally got it out of her that she came here. She didn't want us to know, she was dead against it, and she wouldn't tell what she came for. Add to that the fact that whenever you are remotely connected with anyone who is remotely connected with a murder you always know everything, and there's no question about my needing to know what you were consulted about. I came to ask you myself because I know what you're like."

Wolfe broke his vow. He spoke. "Is Miss Nieder under arrest?"

The phone rang before Cramer could answer. I took it, a voice asked to speak to Inspector Cramer, and Cramer came to my desk and talked. Or rather, he listened. About all he used was grunts, but at one point he said "Here?" with an inflection that started my mind going, and simple logic carried it on to a conclusion.

So as Cramer hung up I pushed in ahead of him to tell Wolfe. "Answering your question, she is not under arrest. They turned her loose because they didn't have enough to back up anything stiffer than material witness, and they put a tail on her, and the tail phoned in that she came here, and the call Cramer just got was a relay on the tail's report. She's in the front room. I put her there because I know how you are about having your meals interrupted. Shall I bring her in?"

Cramer returned to the red leather chair, sat, and said to someone, "You snippy little bastard." I ignored it, knowing it couldn't be for me, since I am just under six feet and weigh a hundred and eighty and therefore could not be called little.

Cramer went at Wolfe. "So the minute we let her go she comes here. That has some bearing on my wanting to know what she was after yesterday, huh?"

Wolfe spoke to me. "Archie. You say Miss Nieder is in the front room?"

"Yes, sir."

"It was she who rang the bell while Mr. Cramer was trying to knock my luncheon dishes off the table?"

"Yes, sir."

"What did she say?"

"Nothing, except that she wanted to see you. She has spent hours with cops and her tongue's tired."

"Bring her in here."

Cramer started offering objections, but I didn't hear him. I went and opened the connecting door to the front room, which was as soundproof as the wall, and said respectfully for all to hear, "Inspector Cramer is here asking about you. Will you come in, please?"

She stood up, hesitated, stiffened herself, and then walked to me and on through. I placed one of the yellow chairs for her, facing Wolfe, closer to my position than to Cramer's. She nodded at me, sat, gave Cramer a straight full look, transferred it to Wolfe, and swallowed.

Wolfe was frowning at her and his eyes were slits. "Miss Nieder," he said gruffly, "I am working for you and you have paid me a retainer. Is that correct?"

She nodded, decided to wire it for sound, and said, "Yes, certainly."

"Then first some advice. The police could have held you as a material witness and you would have had to get bail. Instead, they let you go to give you an illusion of freedom, and they are following you around. Should you at any time want to go somewhere without their knowledge, there's nothing difficult about it. Mr. Goodwin is an expert on that and can tell you what to do."

Cramer was unimpressed. He had got out a cigar and was rolling it between his palms. I never understood why he did that, since you roll a cigar to make it draw better, and he never lit one but only chewed it.

"I understand," Wolfe continued, "that Mr. Cramer and his men have dragged it out of you that you came here yesterday, but that you have refused to tell them what for. Is that correct?"

"Yes."

"Good. I think that was sensible. You are suspected of murder, but that puts you under no compulsion to disclose all the little secrets you have locked up. We all have them, and we don't surrender them if we can help it. But my position in this is quite different from yours. It is true you have hired me, but I am not an attorney-at-law, and therefore what you said to me was not a privileged communication. In my business I need to have the good will, or at least the tolerance, of the police, in order to keep my license to work as a detective. I cannot afford to be intransigent with a police inspector. Besides, I respect and admire Mr. Cramer and would like to help him. I tell you all this so that you will not misunderstand what I am about to do."

Cynthia opened her mouth, but Wolfe pushed a palm at her, and no words came. He turned to Cramer.

"Since your army has had several hours to poke into corners, you have learned, I suppose, that Mr.

Goodwin went to that place yesterday and sat through a show."

"Yeah, I know about that."

"You didn't mention it."

"I hadn't come to it."

"Your reserves?" Wolfe smiled, as mean a smile as I had ever seen. "Well. You heard what I just told Miss Nieder. She came yesterday morning to consult me about her uncle."

"Yeah? What uncle?"

"Mr. Paul Nieder. He is dead. Miss Nieder inherited half of that business from him. Back files of newspapers will tell you that he committed suicide a little over a year ago by jumping into a geyser in Yellowstone Park. Miss Nieder told me about that and many other things—the present status of the business, her own position in it, the deaths of her uncle's former partner and his wife, and so on. I don't remember everything she said, and I don't intend to try. Anyhow it was a *mélange* of facts which your men can easily collect elsewhere. The only thing I can furnish that might help you is the conclusion I formed. I concluded that Miss Nieder had herself pushed her uncle into the geyser, murdered him, and had become fearful of exposure, and had come to me with the fantastic notion of having me get her out of it."

"Why you—" Cynthia was sputtering. "You—"

"Shut up," Wolfe snapped at her. He turned. "Archie. Was that the impression you got?"

"Precisely," I declared.

Cynthia had done fine, I thought, by shutting up as instructed, but I would have risked a wink at her, or at least a helpful glance, if Cramer's eyes hadn't been so comprehensive.

"Thanks for the conclusion," Cramer growled. "Did she tell you that? That she had killed her uncle?"

"Oh, no. No, indeed."

"Exactly what did she want you to do?"

Wolfe smiled the same smile. "That's why I came to that conclusion. She left it very vague about what I was to do. I couldn't possibly tell you."

"Try telling me what you told Goodwin to do when you sent him up there."

Wolfe frowned and called on me. "Do you remember, Archie?"

"Sure I remember." I was eager to help. "You told me to keep a sharp lookout and report everything that happened." I beamed at Cramer. "Talk about the dancers of Bali! Did you ever sit and watch six beautiful girls prancing—"

"You're a goddam liar," he rasped at Wolfe.

Wolfe's chin went up an eighth of an inch. "Mr. Cramer," he said coldly, "I'm tired of this. Mr. Goodwin can't throw you out of here once you're in, but we can leave you here and go upstairs, and you know the limits of your license as well as I do."

He pushed back his chair and was on his feet. "You say I'm lying. Prove it. But for less provocation than you have given me by your uncivilized conduct in my dining room, I would lie all day and all night. Regarding this murder of a bearded stranger, where do I fit, or Mr. Goodwin? Pah. Connect us if you can! Should you be rash enough to constrain us as material witnesses, we would teach you something of the art of lying, and we wouldn't squeeze out on bail; we would dislocate your nose with a habeas corpus ad subjiciendum."

His eyes moved. "Come, Miss Nieder. Come, Archie."

He headed for the door to the hall, detouring around the red leather chair, and I followed him, gathering Cynthia by the elbow as I went by. I presumed we were bound for the plant rooms, which were three flights up, and as we entered the hall I was wondering whether all three of us could crowd into Wolfe's personal elevator without losing dignity. But that problem didn't have to be solved. I was opening my mouth to tell Wolfe that Cynthia and I would use the stairs when here came Cramer striding by. Without a glance at us or a word he went to the front door, opened it, crossed the sill to the stoop, and banged the door shut.

I stepped to the door and put the chain bolt in its slot. Any city employee arriving with papers would have only a two-inch crack to hand the papers through.

Wolfe led us back to the office, motioned us to our chairs, sat at his desk, and demanded of Cynthia, "Did you kill that man?"

She met his eyes and gulped. Then her head went down, her hands went up, her shoulders started to shake, and sounds began to come.

VI

That was terrible. The only thing that shakes Wolfe as profoundly as having a meal rudely interrupted is a bawling woman. His reaction to the first is rage, to the second panic.

I tried to reassure him. "She'll be all right. She just has to—"

"Stop her," he muttered desperately.

I crossed to her, yanked her hands away, using

muscle, pulled her face up, and kissed her hard and good on the lips. She jerked her face aside, shoved at me, and protested, "What the hell!"

That sounded better, and I turned to Wolfe and told him reproachfully, "You can't blame her. I doubt if it's fear or despair or anything normal like that. It's probably hunger. I'll bet she hasn't had a bite since breakfast."

"Good heavens." His eyes popped wide open. "Is that true, Miss Nieder? Haven't you had lunch?"

She shook her head. "They kept me there—and then I had to see you—"

Wolfe was pushing the button. Since it was only five steps from the office to the kitchen door, in seconds Fritz was there.

"Sandwiches and beer at once," Wolfe told him. "Beer, Miss Nieder?"

"I don't have to eat."

"Nonsense. Beer? Claret? Milk? Brandy?"

"Scotch and water. I could use that."

Which of course halted progress for a good twenty minutes. It wasn't only his own meals that Wolfe insisted on safeguarding from extraneous matters. When Fritz brought the tray Cynthia wasn't reluctant about the Scotch, but she needed urging on the sandwiches and got it from both of us. After a taste of the homemade pâté no further urging was required. To make her feel that she could take her time Wolfe conversed with me about the plant germination records. Not about Cramer. His feelings about Cramer were much too warm and too recent. When she was through I put the tray on the table by the big globe, leaving her a glass full of her mixture, and then resumed my seat at my desk.

Wolfe was regarding her warily. "Do you feel better?"

"Much better, yes. I guess I was pretty empty."

"Good." Wolfe leaned back and sighed. "Now. You came to me as soon as the police let you go. Does that mean that you want my help in this new circumstance?"

"It certainly does. I want—"

"Excuse me. We'll go faster if I lead, and Mr. Cramer is quite capable of sending men here with warrants. Let's compress it. There are two points on which I must be satisfied before we can proceed. First, whether you killed that man. An attorney may properly work for a murderer, but I'm not an attorney, and anyway I don't like money from murderers. Did you kill him?"

"No. I want to—"

"Just the no will do if it's the truth. Is it?"

"Yes. It's no."

"I'm inclined to accept it, for reasons mostly not communicable. Some are. For instance, if you had been unable to eat that pâté—" Wolfe cut himself off and sent his eyes at me. "Archie. Did Miss Nieder kill that man?"

I looked at her, my lips puckered, and her gaze met mine. I must admit that she looked pretty ragged, not at all the same person as the one who had modeled, just twenty-four hours before, a dancing dress of Swiss eyelet organdy with ruffled shoulders. She had sure been through something, but not necessarily a murder.

I shook my head and told Wolfe, "No, sir. No guarantee with sanctions, but I vote no. My reasons are like yours, but I might mention that I strongly doubt if I would have had the impulse to make her stop crying by kissing her thoroughly if she had jabbed a window pole into a man's face more than a dozen times. No."

Wolfe nodded. "Then that's settled. She didn't, unless we get cornered by facts, and in that case we'll deserve it. The other point, Miss Nieder, is this: Was the man you saw up there a week ago today your uncle, and was it he who was killed last night?"

A "yes" popped out of her. She added, "It was Uncle Paul. I saw him. I went—"

"Don't dash ahead. We'll get to that. Since I'm assuming your good faith, tentatively at least, I am not suggesting that what you told me yesterday was flummery. I grant that you thought it was your uncle you saw a week ago today, and I accepted it then, but now it's too flimsy for me. You'll have to give me something better if you've got it. What was it that convinced you it was your uncle?"

"I *knew* it was," Cynthia declared. "Maybe if I tried I could tell you how I knew, but I don't have to because now I do know so I could prove it. I've been trying to tell you. You remember what I said about my uncle's private file—that I thought Jean Daumery had taken it and that Bernard has it now. I went there last night to look for it, and saw that—that dead man there on the floor. You can imagine—"

She stopped and made a gesture.

"Yes, I can imagine," Wolfe agreed. "Go ahead."

"I made myself go close to look at him—his face was dreadful but he had the beard and the slick hair. I wanted to do something but I didn't have nerve enough, and I had to sit down to pull myself together. Now they say I was in there fifteen minutes, but I wouldn't think it took me that long to get up my nerve, but maybe it did, and then I went and pulled up the right leg of his trousers and pulled his sock down. He had two little scars about four inches above the ankle, and I knew those scars—that's where my uncle got bit by a dog once. I looked at them close. I had to sit down again—" She stopped, with her mouth open. "Oh! That's why it was fifteen minutes! I had forgotten all about that, sitting down again—"

"Then you left? What did you do?"

"I went home to my apartment and phoned Mr. Demarest. I hadn't—"

"Who's Mr. Demarest?"

"He's a lawyer. He was a friend of Uncle Paul's, and he's the executor. I hadn't told him about seeing my uncle last week because after all I had no proof, and I wanted to find my uncle and talk with him first, so I decided to get you to find him for me. But when I got home I thought the only thing to do was to phone Mr. Demarest, so I did, but he had gone out—"

"Confound it," Wolfe grumbled, "why didn't you phone me?"

"Well—" Cynthia looked harassed. "I didn't know you, did I? Well enough for that? How could I tell what you would believe and what you wouldn't?"

"Indeed," Wolfe said sarcastically. "So you decided to keep it from me, running the risk that I might glance at a newspaper. What is the lawyer doing? Reading up?"

She shook her head. "I didn't get him. I phoned again at eleven-thirty, thinking he would be home by then, but he wasn't, and the state I was in it didn't even occur to me to leave word for him to call. Intending to phone again at midnight, I lay down on the couch to wait, and then—it may be hard to believe but I went to sleep and didn't wake up until nearly seven o'clock. I thought it over and decided not to tell Mr. Demarest or anybody else. During a show season there are lots of people going up and down in those elevators in that building after hours, and I thought they wouldn't remember about me, and my name wasn't in the book because they know me so well and they're not strict about it. That was dumb, wasn't it?"

Wolfe acquiesced with a restrained groan.

She finished the story. "Of course I had to go to work as if nothing had happened. It wasn't easy, but I did, and the place was full of people, police and detectives, when I got there. I had only been there a few minutes when they took me to a fitting room to ask questions, and like a fool I told them I hadn't been there last night when they already knew about it."

Cynthia fluttered a hand. "When they were through with me I phoned Mr. Demarest's office and he was out at lunch. So I came here."

VII

Wolfe heaved a sigh that filled his whole interior. "Well." He opened his eyes and half closed them again. "You said you want my help in this new circumstance. What do you want me to do? Keep you from being convicted of murder?"

"Convicted?" Cynthia goggled at him. "Of murdering my uncle?" Her chin hinges began to give. "I wouldn't—"

"Lay off," I growled at Wolfe, "unless you want to make me kiss her again. She's not a crybaby, but your direct approach is really something. Use synonyms."

"She's not hungry again, is she?" he demanded peevishly. But he eased it. "Miss Nieder. If you're on the defense and intend to stay there, get a lawyer. I'm no good for that. If you want your uncle's murderer caught, whoever it is, and doubt whether the police are up to it, get me. Which do you want, a lawyer or me?"

"I want you," she said, her chin okay.

Wolfe nodded in approval of her sound judgment. "Then we know what we're doing." He glanced at the wall clock. "In twenty minutes I must go up to my orchids. I spend two hours with them every afternoon, from four to six. The most urgent question is this: Who knows that the murdered man was Paul Nieder? Who besides you?"

"Nobody," she declared.

"As far as you know, no one has said or done anything to indicate knowledge or suspicion of his identity?"

"No. They all say they never saw him before, and they have no idea how he got there or who he is. Of course—the way his face was—you wouldn't expect—"

"I suppose not. But we'll assume that whoever killed him knew who he was killing; we'd be donkeys if we didn't. Also we'll assume that he thinks no one else knows. That gives us an advantage. Are you sure you have given no one a hint of your recognition of your uncle last week?"

"Yes, I'm positive."

"Then we have that advantage too. But consider this: if that body is buried without official identification as your uncle, your possession of your inheritance may be further delayed. Also this: you cannot claim the body and give it appropriate burial. Also this: if the police are told who the murdered man was they may be able to do a better job."

"Would they believe—would they keep it secret until they caught him?"

"They might, but I doubt it. Possibly they would fancy the theory that you had killed him in order to hold onto half of that business, and if so your associates up there would be asked to confirm the identification. Certainly Mr. Demarest would be. That's one reason why I shall not tell the police. Another one is that I wouldn't tell Mr. Cramer anything whatever, after his behavior today. But you can do as you please. Do you want to tell them?"

"No."

"Then don't. Now." Wolfe glanced at the clock. "Do you think you know who killed your uncle?"

Cynthia looked startled. "Why no, of course not!"

"You have no idea at all?"

"No!"

"How many people work there?"

"Right now, about two hundred."

"Pfui." Wolfe scowled. "Can any of them get in after hours?"

"No, not unless they have a key—or are let in by someone who has a key. Up to the time of the press showing, even up to yesterday, the first buyers' show, there were people there every evening in the rush of getting the line ready, but most times there's no one there after hours. That's why I picked last night to go to look for that file."

"There was no one working there last night?"

"No, not a soul."

"Who has keys?"

"Let's see." She concentrated. "I have one. Bernard Daumery. . . . Polly Zarella. . . . Ward Roper. That's—oh no, Mr. Demarest has one. As my uncle's executor he is in legal control of the half-interest."

"Who opens up in the morning and locks up at night?"

"Polly Zarella. She has been doing that for years, since before I came there."

"So there are just five keys?"

"Yes, that's all."

"Pah. I can't depend on you. I myself know of two you haven't mentioned. Didn't your uncle have one? He probably let himself in with it last night. And didn't Jean Daumery have one?"

"I was telling about the ones that are there now," Cynthia said with a touch of indignation. "I suppose Uncle Paul had one, of course. I don't know about Jean Daumery's, but if he had it in his clothes that day fishing it's at the bottom of the ocean, and if he didn't have it I suppose Bernard has it now."

Wolfe nodded. "Then we know of four people with keys beside you. Miss Zarella, Mr. Daumery, Mr. Roper, Mr. Demarest. Can you have them here this evening at half-past eight?"

Cynthia gawked. "You mean—here?"

"At this office."

"But good lord." She was flabbergasted. "I can't just order them around! What can I say? I can't say I want them to help find out who killed my uncle because they don't know it was my uncle! You must consider they're much older than I am—all but Bernard —and they think I'm just a fresh kid. Even Bernard is seven years older. After all, I'm only twenty-one— that is, I will be—my God!"

She looked horror-struck, as if someone had poked a window pole at her.

"What now?" Wolfe demanded.

"Tomorrow's my birthday! I'll be twenty-one tomorrow!"

"Yes?" Wolfe said politely.

"Happy birthday!" she cried.

"Not this one," Wolfe stated.

"Look out," I warned him. "That's one of a girl's biggest dates."

He pushed his chair back hastily, arose, and looked at me.

"Archie. I would like to see those people this evening. Six o'clock would do, but I prefer eight-thirty, after dinner. Go up there with Miss Nieder. She is under suspicion of murder, and has engaged me, and can reasonably expect their co-operation. She is in fact half-owner of that business, and one of them is her partner, one is her lawyer, and the other two are her employees. What better do you want?"

He made for the door, on his way to the elevator.

VIII

One of my little notions—that I had already exchanged words with Bernard Daumery—turned out to be wrong. Evidently it is not a Seventh Avenue custom for half-owners to act as doortenders at buyers' shows. At least, contrary to my surmise, it had not been Bernard Daumery who on Monday afternoon had barred Driscoll's Emporium and had given me a head-to-foot survey before letting me in. I never saw that number again.

Business as usual is one of the few things that the

Police Department makes allowances for in handling a homicide. The wheels of commerce must not be stalled unless it is unavoidable. So at the Daumery and Nieder premises eight hours after the discovery of the body, a pug-nosed dick hovering inside near the entrance was the only visible hint that this was the scene of the crime. The city scientists had done all they could and got all that was gettable and had departed. As Cynthia and I entered, the dick recognized me and wanted to know how come, and I told him amiably that I was working for Nero Wolfe and Mr. Wolfe was working for Miss Nieder, pausing just long enough not to seem boorish. I wasn't worried about Cramer. He knew damn well that if he took drastic steps Wolfe would perform exactly as outlined, and that he had been a plain jackass not to wait until Wolfe had downed the other two rice cakes and had some coffee. If the case got really messy and made him desperate he might explode something, but not today or tomorrow.

Cynthia and I were sitting in Bernard Daumery's office, waiting for him to finish with some customers in the showroom. It had been his uncle Jean's room, and was large, light, and airy, with good rugs and furniture, and the walls even more covered with drawings and photographs than in the showroom. We had decided to start with Bernard.

"The trouble with him," Cynthia was telling me with a frown, "is that he can't bear to decide anything. Especially if it's important, you might think he had to wait to see what the stars say or maybe a crystal ball. Then when he does make up his mind he's as stubborn as a mule. The way I do when I want him to agree about something, I act as if it wasn't very important—"

The door came open and a man was there. He shut the door and approached her.

"I'm sorry, Cynthia, it was Miss Dougherty of Bullock's-Wilshire, and Brackett was with her. She thinks you're better than ever, and she's lost her head completely over those three—Oh! Who—?"

"Mr. Goodwin of Nero Wolfe's office," Cynthia told him. "Mr. Daumery, Mr. Goodwin."

I got up to offer a hand and he took it.

"Nero Wolfe the detective?" he asked.

I told him yes. His exuberance about Miss Dougherty of Bullock's-Wilshire evaporated without a trace. He sent Cynthia a look, shook his head, though not apparently at her, went to a chair, not the one at his desk, and sat. Cynthia's statistics had informed me that he was four years younger than me, and I might as well concede them to him. On account of the intimate way he had beamed at Cynthia on entering, naturally I looked upon him as a rival, but to be perfectly fair to him he was built like a man, he knew where to get clothes and how to wear them, and he was not actually ugly.

Now the exuberance was gone. "This godawful mess," he glummed. "Where does Nero Wolfe come in?"

"I went to see him," Cynthia said. "I've hired him."

"What for? To do what?"

"Well—I need somebody, don't I? After the way the police acted with me? When they know I came here last night and apparently no one else did?"

"But that's absolutely idiotic! Why shouldn't you come here?"

"All right, I should. But I think they came within an inch of arresting me."

"Then you need a lawyer. Where's Demarest? Did he send you to Nero Wolfe?"

Cynthia shook her head. "I haven't seen him, but I'm going to as soon as—"

"Damn it, you should have seen him first!"

"I'm not taking your time," Cynthia declared, "to ask you what I should have done. I'll tend to that, thank you. I want to ask you to do something."

I thought she was making a bad start and needed help. "May I join in?" I inquired pleasantly.

Bernard scowled at me. "This thing is absolutely crazy," he complained. "What we ought to do is ignore it! Simply ignore it!"

"Yeah," I agreed, "that would be innocent and brave, but it might get complicated. If one of you gets charged with murder and locked up it would take a master ignorer—"

"Good God, why should we? How could we? Why would any of us kill a man we never saw or heard of before? The thing for the police to do is find out how he ever got in here—that's their problem."

"I completely agree," I assured him heartily. "The trouble is you've got a logical mind and some cops haven't. So the fact remains that one of you, especially one of you that has a key to this place, is apt to get arrested for murder, and right now the odds strongly favor Miss Nieder because they know she used her key last night. Getting convicted is something else, but she would rather not even be arrested right in the middle of the showings of the fall line. May I go on a minute?"

"We're busy as the devil," Bernard muttered.

"I'll be brief. Miss Nieder has hired Mr. Wolfe. She will consult her lawyer, Demarest, within the hour. But meanwhile—"

The door swung open and a man entered. He too shut the door behind him, half turning to close it gently, and then spoke as he advanced.

"Good afternoon, Cynthia. Good afternoon, Bernard. What on earth is going on here?" He saw me. "Who are you, sir, an officer of the law? So am I, in a way. My name is Demarest—Henry R. Demarest, Counselor." He was coming to me to shake on it, and I stood up and obliged.

"Goodwin, Archie," I said, "assistant to Nero Wolfe, private detective."

"Oho!" His brows went up. "Nero Wolfe, eh?" He turned to the others and I had his broad back and the pudgy behind of his neck. "What is all this? A dead man found on the premises and I have to learn it from a policeman asking me about my key? May I ask why I was not informed?"

"We were busy," Bernard said gruffly. "And not with business. The whole police force was here."

"I tried to phone you last night," Cynthia said, "but you weren't at home, and today you were out at lunch, and I have arranged with Nero Wolfe to keep me from being convicted of murder, and Mr. Goodwin came here with me. I was nearly arrested because I came here last night and stayed fifteen minutes."

Demarest nodded. He had deposited his hat on Bernard's desk and his fanny on Bernard's chair the other side of the desk, which seemed a little arbitrary. He nodded again at Cynthia.

"I know. A friend at the District Attorney's office has given me the particulars. But my dear child, you should have called on me at once. I should have been beside you! You went to Nero Wolfe instead? Why?"

He irritated me. Also Cynthia sent me a glance

which I interpreted to mean that hired help are supposed to earn their pay, so I horned in.

"Maybe I can answer that, Mr. Demarest. In fact that's what I was about to do when you entered. You know how it stands now, do you?"

"I know how it stood thirty minutes ago."

"Then you're up with us. I was explaining to Mr. Daumery that Miss Nieder would prefer not to be arrested. Primarily that's what sent her to Mr. Wolfe. I was going on to explain what she can expect of Mr. Wolfe. She won't have to pay him for an all-out job. On a case like this that would mean checking on everybody who entered or left the building last evening after hours, which would be quite a chore itself, considering how careless elevator men get. Things like that are much better left to the police, and a lot of similar jobs, for instance the fingerprint roundup, the laboratory angles, checking alibis, and so on. Naturally the five people who have keys to this place are special cases. Their alibis will get it good, and they'll be tailed day and night, and all the rest of it. We'll let the city pay for all that, not Miss Nieder. That's what Mr. Wolfe won't do."

"It doesn't leave much, does it?" Demarest inquired.

"Enough to keep him occupied. Apparently you've heard of him, Mr. Demarest, so you probably know he goes about it his way. That's what he's doing now, and that's why I'm here. He sent me to arrange a little meeting at his office tonight. Miss Nieder, Miss Zarella, Mr. Daumery, Mr. Roper, and you. You are the five who have keys. Half-past eight would suit him fine if it would suit you. Refreshments served."

Bernard and Demarest made noises. The one from

Bernard was an impatient grunt, but the one from Demarest sounded more like a chuckle.

"We're summoned," the lawyer said.

I grinned at him. "I wouldn't dream of putting it that way."

"No, but we are." He chuckled again. "We who have keys. I offer a comment. You said that Wolfe's primary function, as Miss Nieder sees it, is to prevent her arrest. Obviously he intends to perform it by getting someone else arrested—and tried and convicted. That may prove to be a difficult and expensive undertaking, and possibly quite unnecessary. I would engage, with the situation as it is now, to get the same result with one-tenth the effort and at one-tenth the expense. It's only fair to her, isn't it, to give her that alternative?"

He turned. "It's your money, Cynthia. What about it? Do you want to pay Wolfe to do it his way?"

For a second I thought she was weakening. But she was only deciding how to put it.

"Yes, I do," she declared firmly. "I never had a detective working for me before, and if you can't hire a detective when you're suspected of murder when can you hire one?"

Demarest nodded. "I thought so," he said in a satisfied tone. "Just what I thought. Did you say eight-thirty, Goodwin?"

"That would be best. Mr. Wolfe works better when he isn't looking forward to a meal. You'll come?"

"Certainly I'll come. To save energy. I like to economize on energy, and it will take less to attend that meeting than it would to argue Miss Nieder out of it." He smiled at her. "My dear child! I want a private talk with you."

"Maybe it can wait a few minutes?" I suggested. "Until I finish arranging this? How about it, Mr. Daumery? You'll be with us?"

Bernard was sunk in gloom or something—anyhow, he was sunk. He was hunched in his chair, his eyes going from Cynthia to Demarest to me to Cynthia.

"Okay?" I prodded him.

"I don't know," he muttered. "I'll think it over."

Cynthia emitted a little snort.

Demarest regarded Bernard with exasperation. "As usual. You'll think it over. What is there to think about?"

"There's this business to think about," Bernard declared. "It's bad enough already, with a murdered man found here in the office. We would practically be admitting our connection with it, wouldn't we, the five of us going to discuss it with a detective?"

"I've hired the detective personally," Cynthia snapped.

"I know you have, Cynthia." His tone implied that he was imploring her to make allowances for the air spaces in his skull. "But damn it, we have to consider the business, don't we? It may be inadvisable. I don't know."

"How long would you need to think?" I asked pleasantly. "It's five o'clock now, so there isn't a lot of time. Say an hour and a half? By six-thirty?"

"I suppose so." He sounded uncertain. He looked around at us as if he were a woodchuck in a hole and we were terriers digging to get him. "I'll let you know. Where'll you be?"

"That depends," I replied for us. "There are two more to invite—Miss Zarella and Mr. Roper. It might help if you would get them in here. Would that require thinking over too?"

Demarest chuckled. Cynthia sent me a warning glance, to caution me against aggravating him.

Bernard retorted with spirit. "You do your thinking and I'll do mine." He got up and went to his desk. "Would you mind using another chair, Mr. Demarest?"

Demarest moved out. Bernard sat down and picked up the phone transmitter, and told it, "Please ask Mr. Roper and Miss Zarella to come in here."

I X

They entered together.

I had seen Polly Zarella before. It was she who, the preceding afternoon, had emerged from the door on the left and given the signal that started the show. She still resembled my mother only in point of age. Her lipstick supply was holding out, and so was her shoulder padding, though she had on a different dress. Seeing her on the street, I would have tagged her for a totally different role from the one she filled— Cynthia having informed me that she was a scissors-and-needle wizard, in charge of all Daumery and Nieder production, and a highly important person.

After I had been introduced Bernard invited them to sit. Then he said, "I'm sorry to take your time, but this day is all shot to hell anyhow. Mr. Goodwin wants to ask you something."

They aimed their eyes at me. I grinned at them engagingly.

"You're busy and I'll cut it short. More trouble and fuss, all on account of a dead man. The cops are making it hot for Miss Nieder because she was here last night and said she wasn't when they first brought it up. Now she's in a fix, and she has hired my boss, Nero Wolfe, to get her out. Mr. Wolfe would like to have a talk with five people, the five who carry keys to this place—the five who are here now. He sent me to ask if you will come to his office this evening at half-past eight. Miss Nieder will of course be there. Mr. Demarest is coming. Mr. Daumery is thinking it over and will let us know later. It will be in the interest of justice, it will help to clear up this muddle and let you get back to work, and it will be a favor to Miss Nieder. Will you come?"

"No," Polly Zarella said emphatically.

"No?" I inquired courteously.

"No," she repeated. "I losed much time today. I will be here all evening with cutters cutting."

"This is pretty important, Miss Zarella."

"I do not think so." She said "zink." "He was here, he is gone, and we forget it. I told that to the policemen and I tell it to you. Miss Nieder is not dangered. If she was dangered I would fight it off with these hands"—she lifted them as claws—"because she is the best designer in America or Europe or the world. But she is not. No."

She got up and started for the door. Cynthia, darting to her feet, intercepted her and caught her by the arm.

"I think you ought to wait," I said, "for Mr. Roper's vote. Mr. Roper?"

Ward Roper cleared his throat. "It doesn't seem to me," he offered, in the sort of greasy voice that makes me want to take up strangling, "that this is exactly the proper step to take, under the circumstances."

Seeing that Polly's exit was halted, I was looking

at Roper. Getting along toward fifty, by no means too old to strangle, he was slender, elegant, and groomed to a queen's taste if you let him pick the queen. His voice fitted him to a T.

"What's wrong with it?" I asked him.

He cocked his head to one side to contemplate me. "Almost everything, I would say. I understand and sympathize with Mr. Daumery's desire to think it over. It assumes that we, the five of us, are involved in this matter, which is ridiculous. One may indeed be involved, deeply involved, but not the other four. Not the rest of us."

"What the hell are you getting at?" Bernard demanded with heat.

"Nothing, Bernard. Nothing specific. Just a comment expressing my reaction."

Plainly it was no time for diplomacy. I arose and stepped to a spot nearer Cynthia, where I could face them all without neck-twisting.

"This is a joke," I declared offensively, "and if you ask me, a rotten one." I focused on Bernard. "Have you got around to your thinking, Mr. Daumery? Made up your mind?"

"Certainly not!" He resented it. "Who do you think you are?"

"Just at present I'm Miss Nieder's hired man." My eyes went around. "You're acting, all but Demarest, like a bunch of halfwits! Who do I think I am? Who do you think Miss Nieder is, some little girl asking you to please be nice and help her out? You damn fools, she owns half of this outfit!" I looked at Bernard. "Who are you? You're her business partner, fifty-fifty, and what couldn't she do to you if she felt like it! So you say you'll think it over! Nuts!" I looked at Polly and

Roper. "And what are you? You're her employees, her hired help. She owns half of this firm that you work for. And through me she makes a sensible and reasonable request, and listen to you! As for you, Roper, I hear that you're a good imitator and adapter. I understand that you, Miss Zarella, are as good as they come at producing the goods. But you're not indispensable —neither or both of you. In this affair Mr. Wolfe and I are acting for Miss Nieder. Speaking as her representative, I hereby instruct you to report at the office of Nero Wolfe, Nine-twenty-four West Thirty-fifth Street, at half-past eight this evening."

I wheeled and got Cynthia's eye. "You confirm that, Miss Nieder?"

Her yes was creaky. There was a tadpole in her throat, and she got rid of it and repeated, "Yes. I confirm it."

"Good for you." I turned. "You'll be there, Miss Zarella?"

Polly was staring at me with what seemed to be wide-eyed admiration, but I could be wrong. "But certainly," she said, fully as emphatically as she had previously said no. "If it is so exciting as you make it I will be there with bells on."

"Fine. You, Mr. Roper?"

Roper was chewing his lip. No doubt it was hard for a man of his eminence to swallow a threat of being fired.

"The way you put it," he told me, with a strong suggestion of a tremble in his greasy voice, "I hardly know what to say. It is true, of course, that at some future time Miss Nieder will probably own a half-interest in this business, in the success of which I have had some part for the past fourteen years. That is, she will if she is—available."

"What do you mean, available?"

"Isn't it obvious?" He spread out his hands. "Of course your job is to get her out of it, so you can't be expected to take an objective attitude. But the police are usually right about these things, and you know what they think." The grease suddenly got acutely bitter. "So I merely ask, what if she's not available? As for your—"

What stopped him was movement by Bernard. Cynthia's partner had left his chair and taken four healthy strides to the one occupied by Roper. Roper, startled, got erect in a hurry, nearly knocking his chair over.

"I warned you last night, Ward," Bernard said as if he meant it. "I told you to watch your nasty tongue." His hands were fists. "Apologize to Cynthia, and do it quick."

"Apologize? But what did I—"

Bernard slapped him hard. I couldn't help approving of my rival's good taste in making it a slap, certainly better than my strangling idea, and to spend a solid punch on him would have been flattering him. The first slap teetered Roper's head to the left, and a second one, harder if anything, sent it the other way.

A thought struck me. "Don't fire him!" I called. "Miss Nieder doesn't want him fired! She wants him there tonight!"

"He'll be there," Bernard said grimly, without turning. He had backed up a step to glare at Roper. "You'll be there, Ward, understand?"

That sounded swell, so I crowded my luck. "You will too, Mr. Daumery, won't you?"

What the hell, it was a cinch, with him ordering Roper to come. But he turned around to tell me, "I'll decide later. I'll let you know. I'll phone you. Your number's in the book?"

Demarest chuckled.

X

I like to keep my word, and having on the spur of the moment promised refreshments, they were there. On the table near the big globe were tree-ripened olives, mahallebi, three bowls of nuts, and a comprehensive array of liquids ranging from Wolfe's best brandy down to beer. Each of the guests had a little table at his elbow. At a quarter to nine, when the last arrival had been ushered in, Bernard Daumery and Ward Roper had nothing on their tables but their napkins, Cynthia had Scotch and water, Demarest a Tom Collins, and Polly Zarella a glass and a bottle of Tokaji Essencia. Bernard had phoned around seven o'clock that we could expect him.

If the cops were tailing all of them, as they almost certainly were, I thought there must be quite a convention outside on 35th Street.

I had completed, before dinner, an extra fancy job of reporting. Wolfe had wanted all the details of my party-arranging mission at Daumery and Nieder's, both the libretto and the full score, and I had to get it all in and still leave time for questions before Fritz announced dinner, knowing as I did that if we were late to the table and had to hurry Wolfe would be in a bad humor all evening. In my opinion there would be plenty of bad humor to go around without Wolfe contributing a share, which was another reason for keeping my promise on the refreshments.

Since the staging had been left to me I had placed Cynthia in the red leather chair because I liked her there. Polly Zarella had insisted on having the chair nearest to mine, which might have been just her maternal instinct. On her right was Demarest, and then Roper and Bernard. That seemed a good arrangement, since if Bernard took it into his head to do some more slapping he wouldn't have far to go.

"Thank you for coming," Wolfe said formally.

"We had to," Demarest stated. "Your man Goodwin dragooned us."

"Not you, I understand, Mr. Demarest."

"Oh yes, me too. Only I saw the compulsion a little ahead of the others."

Wolfe shrugged. "Anyway, you're here." His eyes swept the arc. "I believe that Mr. Goodwin has explained to you that, guided by inclination and temperament and compelled by circumstances, my field of investigation in a case like this is severely limited. Fingerprints, documentation, minute and exhaustive inquiry, having people followed around—those are not for me. If this murderer can be identified and exposed by such activities as a thorough examination of all entrances and exits of people at that building last evening, which is possible but by no means assured, the police will do the job. They're fairly good at it. I haven't the patience. But I think we might start by clearing up one point: how you spent your time last evening from eight o'clock to midnight. I take it you have told the police, so I hope you will have no objection to telling me in my capacity as Miss Nieder's servant."

Wolfe's eyes fastened on Demarest. "Will you begin, sir?"

The lawyer was smiling. "If your man had asked that question this afternoon it might have simplified matters. I didn't mention it because I saw Miss Nieder wanted us here."

"It's been mentioned now."

"And now I'll simplify it. You want it all, of course. Yesterday afternoon there was a showing of the Daumery and Nieder fall line to buyers. You know about that, since your man was there. It brought a situation to a climax. For two years now—it began even before Paul Nieder's death—Mr. Roper here has been getting increasingly jealous of Miss Nieder's talent as a creative designer. The reactions to this new line have made it evident that she is vastly superior to him—entirely out of his class. What happened at the buyers' show yesterday enraged him. He wanted to quit. Daumery and Nieder still need him and can use him; his services are valuable within the limits of his abilities. It was desirable to calm him down. Mr. Daumery thought it proper to inform me of the matter and ask my help, since I legally represent a half-share in the firm. Last evening, Tuesday, Mr. Daumery, Miss Zarella, and Mr. Roper dined with me in a restaurant and then we all went to Mr. Daumery's apartment to continue our discussion. Mr. Roper wanted a new contract. My wife was with us. We were together continuously, all five of us, from half-past seven to well after midnight."

Demarest smiled. "It does simplify things, doesn't it?"

It simplified me all right. The best my head could do was let in a wild idea about the four of them taking turns with the window pole, presumably with Mrs. Demarest along to keep count of the jabs. That little speech by that lawyer was one of the few things that made me let my mouth hang open in public.

"It does indeed," Wolfe agreed without a quiver. His eyes moved. "You verify that, Mr. Daumery? All of it as told?"

"I do," Bernard said.

"Do you, Miss Zarella?"

"Oh, yes!"

"Do you, Mr. Roper?"

"I do not," Roper declared, his grease oozing bitterness. "To say that Miss Nieder is vastly my superior is absolutely absurd. I have in my possession three books of clippings from *Women's Wear Daily*, *Vogue*, *Harper's Bazaar*, *Glamor*—"

"No doubt," Wolfe conceded. "We'll allow your exception to that part. Do you verify Mr. Demarest's account of what happened last evening?"

"No. There wasn't the slightest necessity of 'calming me down,' as he put it. I merely wanted—"

"Confound it, were you four people together, with Mrs. Demarest, from seven-thirty till after midnight?"

"Yes, we were."

Wolfe grunted. In a moment he grunted again and turned to me.

"Archie. Miss Nieder's glass is empty. So is Mr. Demarest's. See to it, please."

He leaned back, shut his eyes, and began making little circles on the arm of his chair with the tip of his forefinger. He was flummoxed good, his nose pushed right in level with his face.

I performed as host. Since Demarest's requirement was another Tom Collins it took a little time, but Polly Zarella took none at all since she had shown herself capable of pouring the Tokay herself. Apparently the statement about Cynthia's superiority, out loud for people to hear, had made Roper thirsty, for this time he accepted my offer and chose B & B. In between, glances at Wolfe showed that he was working, and working hard, for his lips were pushing out and then pulling in, out and in, out and in. . . .

I finished the replenishing and resumed my seat.

Wolfe half opened his eyes.

"So," he said conversationally, as if he were merely stating a new paragraph with the continuity intact, "naturally the police are specially interested in Miss Nieder, since she alone, of those who have keys, is vulnerable. By the way, Mr. Daumery, how did it happen that Miss Nieder wasn't invited to that conference? Isn't she a half-owner?"

"I represented her interests," Demarest stated.

"But before long she'll probably be representing herself. Shouldn't she be consulted on important matters?"

Bernard spoke. "Damn it, isn't it obvious? If she had been there we couldn't have handled Roper at all. He can't bear the sight of her."

"I deny—" Roper began, but Wolfe cut him off.

"Even so, isn't it true that Miss Nieder has been deliberately and consistently ignored in the management of the business?"

"Yes," Polly said, nodding emphatically.

The three men said no simultaneously, and all were going on to elaborate, but again Wolfe took it away.

"This will finish sooner if you let me dominate it. I am not implying that Miss Nieder is unappreciated. You all admit her designing talent, all but Mr. Roper, and just this afternoon one of you was quick and eager to resent an aspersion on her. I mean, Mr. Daumery, your assaulting Mr. Roper only because he hinted that Miss Nieder might have killed a man. Your business needs him, and surely you were risking losing him. You leaped hot-headed to Miss Nieder's defense. It isn't easy to reconcile that with your reluctance to come here this evening at her request."

"I wasn't reluctant. I had to think it over, that's all."

"You often have to think things over, don't you?"

Bernard resented it. "What's it to you if I do?"

"It's a great deal to me," Wolfe declared. "I have engaged to prevent Miss Nieder's arrest for murder, and I suspect that your habit of thinking things over is going to show me how to do it, and I intend to learn if I'm right."

His gaze shifted. "Mr. Demarest. How long have you known Mr. Daumery?"

"Six years. Ever since he graduated from college and started to work in his uncle's business."

"You've known him intimately?"

"Yes and no. I was an intimate friend of Paul Nieder, the partner of Bernard's uncle."

"Please give me a considered answer to this: has he always had to think things over? Have you noticed any change in him in that respect, at any time?"

Demarest smiled. "I don't have to consider it. He was always a very decisive young man, even aggressive, until he became the active head of the business after his uncle's death some six weeks ago. But that was only natural, wasn't it? A man of his age suddenly taking on so great a responsibility?"

"Perhaps. Miss Zarella, do you agree with what Mr. Demarest has said?"

"Oh, yes!" Polly was emphatic as usual. "Bernard has been so different!"

"And do you, Miss Nieder?"

Cynthia was frowning. "Well, I suppose people might have got that impression—"

"Nonsense," Wolfe bit her off. "You're hedging. Mr. Daumery was ardent in resenting a suspicion that you had committed a murder, but you don't have to reciprocate for him. His alibi is impregnable. Was there a change in Mr. Daumery, as stated, about six weeks ago?"

"Yes, there was, but Mr. Demarest has explained why."

"He thinks he has. Now we're getting somewhere." Wolfe's eyes darted at Bernard. "Mr. Daumery, I wish to ask you some questions as Miss Nieder's agent. They may strike you as irrelevant or even impertinent, but if they are not actually offensive will you answer them?"

Bernard had the look of a man who suspects that someone is sneaking up behind him but for reasons of his own doesn't want to turn and see. "I probably will," he said. "What are the questions?"

"Thank you," Wolfe said graciously. "Are your parents alive?"

"Yes."

"Where are they?"

"In Los Angeles. My father is a professor in the university there."

"Is either of them conversant with your business affairs?"

"Not especially. In a vague general way."

"Have you brothers or sisters?"

"Two younger sisters. In college."

"Have you any other relatives that you see or correspond with frequently?"

Bernard looked at Cynthia. "Do you want me to go on with this autobiography?"

"She has no opinion in the matter," Wolfe said curtly, "because she doesn't know what I'm after. You may or may not have guessed. But can you object that my questions are offensive?"

"No, they're only silly."

"Then humor me—or humor Miss Nieder through me. Any other relatives that you see or correspond with frequently?"

"None whatever."

"I'm about through. I won't name any names, because the only ones I know are already eliminated. For help in making important decisions, manifestly it is not Mr. Demarest you turn to, since he has had to rationalize the change he has noticed in you. Nor Miss Zarella nor Mr. Roper, since their attitude toward Mr. Goodwin's invitation to come here this evening had no effect on yours. I'll have to put it in general terms: is there a banker, or lawyer, or friend, or any other person or persons, on whose judgment you frequently rely for guidance in your business? Anyone at all?"

"No special person. I discuss things with people, naturally—including Mr. Demarest—"

"Ha! Not Mr. Demarest. He has noticed a change in you. This is your last chance, Mr. Daumery, to drag somebody in."

"I don't have to drag anybody in. I'm of sound mind and body and over twenty-one."

"I know you are, and of a decisive and aggressive temperament, and that's why I'm making progress." Wolfe wiggled a finger at him. "One last question. Yesterday Miss Nieder suggested, frivolously I thought, that you might find counsel in the stars or a crystal ball. Do you?"

Bernard croaked at Cynthia, "Where the hell did you get that idea?"

"I said she was being frivolous," Wolfe told him. "Do you? Or tea leaves or a fortune-teller?"

"No!"

Wolfe nodded. "That's all, Mr. Daumery. Thank you again. That satisfies me."

He took them all in. "You have a right to know, I think, who it was that was killed in the Daumery and Nieder office last evening. It was Mr. Paul Nieder, the former partner in the business."

XI

Everybody stared at him. If I had had a pin handy I would have tried dropping it.

"What did you say?" Demarest demanded.

"By my mother's milk," Polly Zarella cried, springing to her feet, "it was! It was Paul! When they made me look at him I saw he had Paul's hands, Paul's wonderful artist hands, only I knew it couldn't be!" At Wolfe's desk, glaring at him ferociously, she drummed on the desk with her fists. "How?" she demanded. "Tell me how!"

I had to get up and help out or she might have climbed over the desk and drummed on Wolfe's belly, which would have stopped the party. The others were reacting too, but not as spectacularly as Polly. My firmness in getting her back in her chair had a quieting effect on them too, and Wolfe's words could come through.

"You'll want to know all about it, of course, and

eventually you will, but right now I have a job to do. Since, as I say, Mr. Nieder was killed last night, it follows that he didn't kill himself over a year ago. He only pretended to. A week ago today Miss Nieder saw him in your showroom, disguised with a beard and glasses and slick parted hair. She recognized him, but he departed before she could speak to him. When she entered that office last evening the body was there on the floor, and she confirmed the identification by recognizing scars on his leg. Further particulars must wait. The point is that this time he was killed indeed, and I think I know who killed him."

His eyes went straight at Bernard.

"Where is he, Mr. Daumery?"

Bernard was not himself. He was trying hard to be but couldn't make it. He was meeting Wolfe's hard gaze with a fascinated stare, as if he were entering the last stage of being hypnotized.

"Where is he?" Wolfe insisted.

The best Bernard could do was a "Who?" that didn't sound like him at all.

Wolfe slowly shook his head. "I'm not putting anything on," he said dryly. "When Mr. Goodwin told me what happened this afternoon this possibility occurred to me, along with many others, but up to half an hour ago, when I got my head battered in by being told that you four people spent last evening together, I had no idea of where my target was. Then, after a little consideration, I decided to explore, and now I know. Your face tells me. Don't reproach yourself. The attack was unexpected and swift and everything was against you."

Wolfe extended a hand with the palm up. "Even if I didn't know, but still only guessed, that would be enough. I would merely give it to the police as a suspicion deserving inquiry, and with their trained noses and their ten thousand men how long do you think it would take them to find him? Another fact that may weigh with you: he is a murderer. Even so, you are a free agent in every respect but one; you will not be permitted to leave this room until either you have told me where he is or I have given the police time to start on his trail and cover my door."

Demarest chuckled. "Unlawful restraint with witnesses," he commented.

Wolfe ignored it and gave the screw another turn on Bernard. "Where is he, Mr. Daumery? You can't take time to think it over, to consult him on this one. Where is he?"

"This is awful," Bernard said hoarsely. "This is an awful thing."

"He can't do this!" came suddenly from the red leather chair. Cynthia's concentrated gaze at Bernard was full of a kind and degree of sympathy that I had hoped never to see her spend on a rival. "He can't threaten you and keep you here! It's unlawful!" Her head jerked to Wolfe and she snapped at him, "You stop it now!"

"It's too late, my dear child," Demarest told her. "You hired him—and I must admit you're getting your money's worth." His head turned. "You'd better tell him, Bernard. It may be hard, but the other way's harder."

"Where is he, Mr. Daumery?" Wolfe repeated.

Bernard's chin lifted a little. "If you're right," he said, still hoarse, "and God knows I hope you're not, it's up to him. The address is Eight-sixteen East Ninetieth Street. I want to phone him."

"No," Wolfe said curtly. "You will be unlawfully

restrained if you try. What is it, an apartment building?"

"Yes."

"Elevator?"

"Yes."

"What floor?"

"The tenth. Apartment Ten C. I rented it for him."

"Is he there now?"

"Yes. I was to phone him there when I left here. I said I would go to see him, but he said I might be followed and I had better phone from a booth."

"What is the name?"

"Dickson. George Dickson."

"That's his name?"

"Yes."

"Thank you. Satisfactory. Archie."

"Yes, sir?"

"Give Fritz a revolver and send him in. I don't know how some of these minds might work. Then get Mr. Dickson and bring him here. Eight-one-six East—"

"Yeah, I heard it."

"Don't alarm him any more than you have to. Don't tell him we know who got killed last night. I don't want you killed, and I don't want a suicide."

"Don't worry," Demarest volunteered, "about *him* committing suicide. What I'm wondering is how you expect to prove anything about a murder. You've admitted that half an hour ago you didn't even know he existed. He's tough and he's anything but a fool."

I was at a drawer of my desk, getting out two guns and loading them—one for Fritz and one for me. So I was still there to hear Ward Roper's contribution.

"That explains it," Roper said, the bitterness all

gone, replaced by a tone of pleased discovery. "If Paul was alive up to last night, he designed those things himself and got them to us through Cynthia! Certainly! That explains it!"

I didn't stay for the slapping, if any.

"There's no hurry," Wolfe told me as I was leaving. "I have things to do before you get back."

XII

For transportation I had my pick of the new Cadillac, the subway, or a taxi. It might not be convenient to have my hands occupied with a steering wheel, and escorting a murderer on a subway without handcuffs is a damn nuisance, so I chose the taxi. The driver of the one I flagged on Tenth Avenue had satisfactory reactions to my license card and my discreet outline of the situation, and I elected him.

Eight-sixteen East Ninetieth Street was neither a dump nor a castle of luxury—just one of the big clean hives. Leaving the taxi waiting at the curb, I entered, walked across the lobby as if I were in my own home, entered the elevator, and mumbled casually, "Ten please."

The man moved no muscle but his jaw. "Who do you want to see?"

"Dickson."

"I'll have to phone up. What's your name?"

"Tell him it's a message from Mr. Bernard Daumery."

The man moved. I followed him out of the elevator and around a corner to the switchboard, and watched him plug in and flip a switch. In a moment he was speaking into the transmitter, and in another moment he turned to me.

"He says for me to bring the message up."

"Tell him my name is Goodwin and I was told to give it to him personally."

Apparently Dickson didn't have to think things over. At least there was no extended discussion. The man pulled out the plug, told me to come ahead, and led me back to the elevator. He took me to the tenth floor and thumbed me to the left, and I went to the end of the hall, to the door marked 10C. The door was ajar, to a crack big enough to stick a peanut in, and as my finger was aiming for the pushbutton a voice came through.

"You have a message from Mr. Daumery?"

"Yes, sir, for George Dickson."

"I'm Dickson. Hand it through to me."

"I can't. It's verbal."

"Then say it. What is it?"

"I'll have to see you first. You were described to me. Mr. Daumery is in a little trouble."

For a couple of seconds nothing happened, then the door opened wide enough to admit ten bags of peanuts abreast. Since he had certainly had his hoof placed to keep it from opening, I evened up by promptly placing mine to keep it from shutting. The light was nothing wonderful, but good enough to see that he was a husky middle-aged specimen with a wide mouth, dark-colored deepset eyes, and a full share of chin.

"What kind of trouble?" he snapped.

"He'll have to tell you about it," I said apologetically. "I'm just a messenger. All I can tell you is that I was instructed to ask you to come to him."

"Why didn't he phone me?"

"A phone isn't available to him right now."

"Where is he?"

"At Nero Wolfe's office on West Thirty-fifth Street."

"Who else is there?"

"Several people. Mr. Wolfe, of course, and men named Demarest and Roper, and women named Zarella and Nieder—that's all."

The dark eyes had got darker. "I think you're lying. I don't think Mr. Daumery sent for me at all. I think this is a put-up job and you can get out of here and stay out."

"Okay, brother." I kept the foot in place. "Where did I get your name and address, from a mailing list? You knew Mr. Daumery was at Nero Wolfe's, since he phoned you around seven o'clock to ask your advice about going, and he told you who else was invited, so what's wrong with that? Why do you think he can't use a phone, because he don't speak English? Even if it were a put-up job as you say, I don't quite see what you can do except to come along and unput it, unless you'd rather do it here. They've got the impression that your help is badly needed. My understanding was that if I didn't get there with you by eleven o'clock they would all pile into a taxi, including Mr. Daumery, and come here to see you. So if you turn me down all I can do is push on inside and wait with you till they arrive. If you try to bounce me, we'll see. If you call on that skinny elevator pilot for help, we'll still see. If you summon cops, I'll try my hardest to wiggle out of it by explaining the situation to them. That seems to cover it, don't you think? I've got a taxi waiting out front."

From the look in his eye I thought it likely that he was destined to take a poke at me, or even make a dash for some tool, say a window pole, to work with. There was certainly no part of me he liked. But, as Demarest had said, he was anything but a fool. Most men would have needed a good ten minutes alone in a quiet corner to get the right answer to the problem this bird suddenly found himself confronted with. Not Mr. Dickson. It took him a scant thirty seconds, during which he stood with his eyes on me but his brain doing hurdles, high jumps, and fancy dives.

He wheeled and opened a door, got a hat from a shelf and put it on, emerged to the hall as I backed out, pulled the door shut, marched to the elevator, and pushed the button.

By the time we had descended to the sidewalk, climbed into the taxi, been driven to Wolfe's address, mounted the stoop and entered, and proceeded to the office, he had not uttered another word. Neither had I. I am not the kind that shoves in where he isn't wanted.

XIII

We were back again to the headline we had started with: MAN ALIVE. This time, however, I did not regard it as a letdown. I took it for granted that by the time I got back everyone there would know who was coming with me, even if one or two of them hadn't caught on before I left. I thought it would be interesting to see how they would welcome, under those difficult circumstances, their former employer and associate on his return from a watery grave, but he took charge of the script himself as he entered the office. He strode across to face Bernard and glare down at him. Bernard scrambled to his feet.

Dickson asked, his tone cold and biting, "What the hell's the matter with you? Can't you handle anything at all?"

"Not this I can't," Bernard said, and he was by no means whimpering. "This man Wolfe is one for you to handle, and I only hope to God you can!"

Without moving his shoulders, Dickson pivoted his head to take them in. "Well, I'm back," he announced. "I would have been back soon anyway, but this bright nephew of mine has hurried it up a little. Ward, you're looking like a window display in a fire sale. Still putting up with them, Polly? Now you'll have to put up with me again. Cynthia, I hear you're on the way to lead the whole pack." His head pivoted some more. "Where's Henry? I thought he was here."

I was asking that question myself. Neither Wolfe nor Demarest was in sight. I had turned to ask Fritz where they were, but he had left the room as soon as I appeared. And not only were those two missing, but what was fully as surprising, there had been two additions to the party. Inspector Cramer and my favorite sergeant, Purley Stebbins, were seated side by side on the couch over in the far corner.

I dodged my way through the welcomers, some sitting and some standing, and asked Cramer respectfully, "Where's Mr. Wolfe?"

"Somewhere with a lawyer," Cramer growled, "making up charades. Who's that you brought in?"

"George Dickson, so I'm told. I suppose Mr. Wolfe phoned you to come and get a murderer?"

"He did."

"Your face is dirty, Purley."

"Go to hell."

"I was just starting. Excuse me."

I began to dodge my way back to the hall door, thinking that I had better find my employer and inform him that I had delivered as usual, but I was only halfway there when he and Demarest appeared, coming in to us. After one swift glance at the assembly, the lawyer sidled off along the wall to a remote chair over by the bookshelves, evidently not being in a welcoming mood. Wolfe headed for his desk, but in the middle of the room found himself blocked. George Dickson was there, facing him.

"Nero Wolfe?" Dickson put out a hand. "I'm Jean Daumery. This is a real pleasure!"

Wolfe stood motionless. The room was suddenly quiet, painfully quiet, and all eyes were going in one direction, at the two men.

"How do you do, Mr. Daumery," Wolfe said dryly, stepped around him, and walked to his chair. Except for the sound of that movement the quiet held. Jean Daumery let his hand fall, which is about all you can do with a rejected hand unless you want to double it into a fist and use it another way. After solving the hand problem, Jean turned a half-circle to face Wolfe's desk and spoke in a different tone.

"I was told that my nephew sent for me. He didn't. You got me here by a trick. What do you want?"

"Sit down, sir," Wolfe said. "This may take all night."

"Not all of my night. What do you want?"

"Sit down and I'll tell you. I want to present some facts, offer my explanation of them, and get your opinion. There's a chair there beside your nephew."

To a man trying to grab the offensive and hold it,

it's a comedown to accept an invitation to be seated. But the alternative, to go on standing in a room full of sitters, is just as awkward, unless you intend to walk out soon, and Jean couldn't know what he intended until he learned what he was up against. He took the chair next to Bernard.

"What facts?" he asked.

"I said," Wolfe told him, "that this may take all night, but that doesn't mean that I want it to. I'll make it as short as possible." He reached to his breast pocket and pulled out folded sheets of paper. "Instead of telling you what this says I'll read it to you." He glanced around. "I suppose you all know, or most of you, that tomorrow will be Miss Nieder's twenty-first birthday."

"Oh, yes!" Polly Zarella said emphatically.

Wolfe glared at her. He couldn't stand emphatic women. "I persuaded Mr. Demarest," he said, "to anticipate the delivery date of this paper by a few hours. It was intended, as you will see, only for Miss Nieder, but, as Mr. Cramer would tell you if you asked him, evidence in a case of murder has no respect for confidences."

He unfolded the paper. "This," he said, "is a holograph. It is written on two sheets of plain bond paper, and is dated at the top Yellowstone Park, May sixteenth, Nineteen forty-six. It starts, 'My dearest Cynthia,' and goes on:

> "I'll send this to Henry, sealed, and tell him not to open it and to give it to you on your twenty-first birthday. That will be June eleventh next year. How I would love to be with you that day! Well, perhaps I will. If I'm not, I think by that time you will know your way around enough to decide for yourself how

to look at this. You ought to know about it, but I
don't want you to right now."

Wolfe looked up. "This is not paragraphed. Evidently Mr. Nieder didn't believe in paragraphs." He
returned to the paper:

"You are going to get the news that I have killed
myself and a farewell note from me. I know that will
affect you, because we are fond of each other in spite
of all our differences, but it won't break your heart.
I'm not going to kill myself. I hope and expect to be
with you again and with the work I love. I'm writing
this to explain what I'm doing. I think you know that
I loved Helen. You didn't like her, and that's one
thing I have against you, because she gave me the
only warm happiness I have ever known outside of
my work. She understood what I—but I don't want
to make this too long. I only want you to know what
happened. Jean found out about us and killed her.
Just how he did it I don't know, but out alone with
her on the horses it would have been easy for a man
like him, with his will power and cleverness. He intended to kill me too, and he still intends to, and as
you know, Jean always does everything he intends
to do. That's why I wouldn't leave the apartment
those three days and nights, and that's why I came
away. I don't suppose I am very brave, at least not
physically brave, and of course you know that Jean
has always overwhelmed me. I was in complete terror of him after he killed Helen, and I still am. He
will not forget and he will never leave anything undone. I'm surprised that he hasn't followed me out
here, and perhaps he has, but he loves his part of
that business nearly as much as I love mine, and the
fall line is being assembled, and I think he'll wait
until I get back. I tore myself away only to save my
life. Only I'm not coming back, not now. When he
gets the news he'll think I'm dead. I can't stay away

forever, I know that. I'll see what happens. He might die himself. People do die. But I'm trying to study what I know of his character. I know him pretty well. I think it is possible that if he thinks of me as dead for a long time, perhaps two or three years or even only one year, and then I suddenly return to join him in that business again and do for it what no one else can do, his mind may work in such a way that he will not feel he has to carry out his intention of killing me. That's one of the possibilities. Anyhow I'll see what happens. I know I can't stay away forever. It may be that somehow I'll be back with you and my work before your twenty-first birthday comes, and if so I'll get this from Henry and you will never see it. But I'll send it to him because if I never do get back I want you to know the truth of this. I'm going to tell you in my farewell note that I am depending on you to keep that business at the top because you have a fine talent, a very fine talent that I'm proud of, and that will be the only part of my farewell note that will not be a fake. I mean every word of that. I am very fond of you and proud of you. Your Uncle Paul."

Wolfe folded the sheets and returned them to his pocket, and looked up.

"It is a capital U in Uncle," he announced.

Polly Zarella and Cynthia both had tears in their eyes.

Polly jumped to her feet, brushing the tears away without bothering about a handkerchief, and faced Jean Daumery with her eyes blazing. "I quit!" she shrieked. "I give you two weeks' notice before people! You said I'll have to put up with you but I won't! There will be a new business, Zarella and Nieder, and Cynthia and I will show you! You and Ward Roper to compete with us? Phut!"

Her spitting at him seemed to be unintentional, merely coming out with the phut.

"Confound it, madam, sit down," Wolfe grumbled.

Polly darted to Cynthia and was apparently going to begin arrangements for the new partnership then and there, but the sound of Jean Daumery's voice sidetracked her.

"I see," Jean said calmly. He had tightened up. "You got me down here to accuse me of murdering my wife, with that hysterical letter from Paul Nieder to back it up. This is absolutely fantastic!"

Wolfe nodded. "It would be," he agreed, "so that's not what I'm doing. I don't waste time on fantasy. I read that letter only for background. To get down to our real business: when and where did you last see Mr. Nieder?"

Jean shook his head. "From fantasy to fact? *Our* business? When and where I did this or that is certainly my business, but not yours. You were going to tell *me* facts."

"You won't answer that?"

"Certainly not, why should I? I don't owe you any answers to anything."

"You're entirely correct," Wolfe conceded, "but not very intelligent. I suppose you know that those two gentlemen on the couch are Police Inspector Cramer and Sergeant Stebbins. Their presence does not mean that I asked that question with the voice of authority, but surely it makes it obvious that if you don't answer me you will be given an opportunity to answer them. Suit yourself. I'll try again. When and where did you last see Mr. Paul Nieder?"

Once more Jean proved himself capable of a swift and sensible decision. "I don't know the exact date," he said, "but it was early in May last year, at our place of business, just before he left for a vacation."

"Aha," Wolfe murmured in a pleased tone, "that's more like it. Now, Mr. Daumery, here are a few of the facts I promised. Mr. Nieder did not kill himself a year ago May; you heard that letter I read. He was seen, alive, here in New York, last week, by his niece, disguised with a beard, slick hair parted on the left side, and glasses. He was seen again this morning, by many people, only this time he was dead. The manner of his death—"

"So that's what you had!" Inspector Cramer was no longer on the couch but right among us—or at least among Wolfe, at his desk, barking at him. "By God, this time you've asked for it!"

"Pfui," Wolfe said peevishly. "I've got Mr. Daumery here for you, haven't I? Do you want to take it over now? Are you ready to? Or shall I give him some more facts?"

Cramer's eyes left Wolfe for a look around. When they hit Cynthia they must have had a message for her, for she left her seat and walked to one over near Demarest. Cramer went and sat in the red leather chair, which put him in the center of things with a full-face view of Jean Daumery. Purley Stebbins had moved too, quietly pulling up a chair to Jean's rear about arm's length off.

"Let's hear your facts," Cramer growled.

Wolfe's gaze was back at Jean. "I was about to say," he resumed, "that the manner of that man's death—no one but his niece knew it was Mr. Nieder— made it necessary to call in the police. They did what they were supposed to do, and naturally they concentrated on the most important point: who was he? As you see, Mr. Daumery, Mr. Cramer resents not being told by the only people who knew—Miss Nieder, Mr. Goodwin, and me—but that's really foolish of him. For if he had known who the dead man was he would probably, and reasonably, have focused on the most likely culprit, Miss Nieder, who was known to have been on the spot and who had the excellent motive of wanting to keep her inheritance of a half-share in the business. As it stood, it was vital for the police to identify the corpse. I don't know, Mr. Daumery, whether you are aware of the stupendous resources of the New York police in attacking a problem like that. You may be sure that they employed all of them in trying to trace that man with a beard and slick hair parted on the left side and glasses. That's one of the facts I ask you to consider. Is it likely that they failed entirely? Is it likely that they found no one, anywhere, who had seen such a man? I am anxious to be quite fair with you. Is it not likely, for instance, that if the bearded man had been seen recently, on the street or in some other public place, talking with another man—say a man whose description tallies well with yours—that the police have learned of it and can produce a witness or witnesses to identify the second man?"

Wolfe raised a finger, and suddenly bent in to aim straight at Jean. "I am fairly warning you. It is nothing against you that you told me you last saw Paul Nieder over a year ago. Nobody likes to be involved in disagreeable matters. But now be careful. If, after what I have just said, you persist in lying, you can't blame us if we surmise—look at his face, Mr. Cramer! Do you see his face?"

Wolfe let the silence work, and the pairs of eyes all fixed on Jean's face, with his finger still nailing the target, for a full five seconds, and then suddenly snapped, like the snap of a whip.

"When and where did you last see Paul Nieder, Mr. Daumery?"   •

It was devilish. No man could have stood up under it completely whole. What was Jean going to do about his face? What was he going to say?

He said nothing.

Wolfe leaned back and let his eyes open to more than slits. "It offers," he said like a lecturer, "a remarkable field for speculation. What, for instance, made you suspect that his suicide was a fake? Possibly you were as well acquainted with his character as he was with yours, and you knew it was extremely improbable that he could jump into a geyser with no clothes on. Indeed, there are few men who could. In any case, he was right about you; you did not forget or abandon your intention. It would have been dangerous to hire someone to find him, and if you undertook it yourself it might have taken years. You decided to coax him out. You went to Florida on a fishing trip with your nephew, and you arranged with him to stage a drowning for you. Another speculation: how much did you tell him? Did you have to let him in—"

"No!"

It was Bernard. He was out of his chair, but not to confront his uncle or to bear down on Wolfe. He had turned to where Cynthia's new position had put her in his rear, and his explosion was for her.

"Get this straight, Cynthia!" he told her. "I'm not trying any scuttle or any sneak, and whatever he has done that's up to him with no pushes from me, but this is my part and you've got to have it straight!" He wheeled to his uncle. "You told me that someone had it in for you and your life was in danger. You said nothing about Paul Nieder, and of course I thought he was dead. You said that your supposed death would force this person to take certain steps and that the situation would soon be changed so that you could reappear. For all I know, that's who it really was. I don't know." He turned back to Cynthia. "I don't know anything, except that I'm damned if I'm going to have you listen to insinuations that I'm mixed up in this."

"Shut up and sit down," his uncle told him.

Bernard wheeled again. Wolfe nodded at him. "Thank you, sir, for relieving us of that speculation. There are plenty left." He looked at Jean. "For example, at that encounter with your disguised former partner, wherever it was and however it came about, did you two arrange to meet Tuesday evening at your place of business to discuss matters and reach an understanding? It must have been an interesting meeting, with him thinking you dead and you supposedly thinking him dead. Did you persuade him that you hadn't killed your wife? And why didn't you kill him somewhere else? Was it bravado, to leave him there, with his mutilated face, on the floor of his own office, or were you afraid to postpone it even for an hour, for fear he would disclose himself to Miss Nieder or Mr. Demarest, and so increase your risk? And why on earth did you jab that thing at him more than a dozen times? Were you hysterical? Surely you didn't think it necessary to prevent his being identified, with everyone thinking him dead long ago."

"It was a wolf tearing a carcass into pieces," Polly Zarella declared emphatically.

"Perhaps." Wolfe's shoulders went up a quarter of an inch and down again. "You can have him, Mr. Cramer. I'm through with him."

Cramer was scowling. "I could use some more facts."

"Bah." Wolfe resented it. "What more do you want? You saw his face; you are seeing it now, with all the time he's had to arrange it. I phoned you that he would be here for you, and there he is. I've done my part and you can do yours. He got into that building last night and out again, and was not invisible. That's really all you need."

Cramer arose. Purley Stebbins was already up.

"One thing I need," said Cramer, stepping to the desk, "is that letter Nieder wrote." He extended a hand. "There in your breast pocket."

Wolfe shook his head. "I'll keep that—or rather, I'll destroy it. It's mine."

"Like hell it is!"

"Certainly it is. It's in my handwriting. I wrote it while Archie was going for him—with Mr. Demarest's help. You won't need it. Just take him out of here and get to work."

XIV

For my own satisfaction I have got to add that this was one time Wolfe outsmarted himself. Not far from the top of the list of the things he abhors is being a witness at a trial, and ordinarily he takes good care to handle things so that he won't get a subpoena. But only last week I had the pleasure of sitting in the courtroom and watching him—and listening to him— in the witness chair. The District Attorney wasn't any too sure of his case, and on this one Wolfe couldn't shake him loose. It was a good thing for Cynthia that Wolfe didn't know what would happen at the time we sent her a bill, or she might have had to hock her half of the business to pay it. Wolfe got sore about it all over again just yesterday morning, when the paper informed him that the jury had stayed out only two hours and forty minutes before bringing in a first-degree verdict. That proved, he claimed, that his testimony hadn't been needed.

The owners of Daumery and Nieder tell me that not only will I be welcome at any of their shows, front row seat, but also that any number I want to pick will be sent with their compliments to any name and address I choose. I thought Cynthia understood me better than that. Women just don't give a damn. I suppose in a month or so she'll be light-heartedly sending me an invitation to the wedding.

Omit Flowers

I

In my opinion it was one of Nero Wolfe's neatest jobs, and he never got a nickel for it.

He might or might not have taken it on merely as a favor to his old friend Marko Vukcic, who was one of the only three people who called him by his first name, but there were other factors. Rusterman's Restaurant was the one place besides home where Wolfe really enjoyed eating, and Marko owned it and ran it, and he put the bee on Wolfe in one of the small private rooms at Rusterman's as the cheese cart was being wheeled in to us at the end of a specially designed dinner. Furthermore, the man in trouble had at one time been a cook.

"I admit," Marko said, reaching to give me another hunk of Cremona Gorgonzola, "that he forfeited all claim to professional respect many years ago. But in my youth I worked under him at Mondor's in Paris, and at the age of thirty he was the best sauce man in France. He had genius, and he had a generous heart. I owe him much. I would choke on this cheese if I sat on my hands while he gets convicted of a murder he did not commit." Marko gestured with the long thin knife. "But who am I? A Boniface. Whereas you are a great detective, and my friend. I appeal to you to save him." Marko pointed the knife at me. "And, naturally, to Archie—also, I hope, my friend."

I nodded with much feeling, having his food and wine all through me. "Absolutely," I agreed, "but don't waste any butter on me. All I do is carry things."

"Ha," Marko said skeptically. "I know how deep you go, my friend. As for the money that will be required, I shall of course furnish it."

Wolfe grunted, drawing our eyes to him. His big face, which never looked big on account of the great expanse of the rest of him, was cheerful and a little flushed, as always after a good meal, but the annoyance that had brought forth the grunt showed in his eyes. They were on our host.

"Pfui." He grunted again. "Is this right, Marko? No. If you want to hire me and pay me, I do business in my office, not at your table. If you want to draw on friendship, why mention money? Do you owe this man —what's his name?"

"Pompa. Virgil Pompa."

"Do you owe him enough to warrant a draft on my affection?"

"Yes." Marko was slightly annoyed too. "Damn it, didn't I say so?"

"Then I have no choice. Come to my office tomorrow at eleven and tell me about it."

"That won't do," Marko declared. "He's in jail, charged with murder. I had a devil of a time getting to him this afternoon, with a lawyer. Danger is breathing down his neck and he's nearly dead of fear. He is sixty-eight years old."

"Good heavens." Wolfe sighed. "Confound it, there were things I wanted to talk about. And what if he killed that man? From the newspaper accounts it seems credible. Why are you so sure he didn't?"

"Because I saw him and heard him this afternoon. Virgil Pompa could conceivably kill a man, of course. And having killed, he certainly would have sense enough to lie to policemen and lawyers. But he could not look me in the eye and say what he said the way he said it. I know him well." Marko crossed his chest with the knife as if it had been a sword. "I swear to you, Nero, he did not kill. Is that enough?"

"Yes." Wolfe pushed his plate. "Give me some more cheese and tell me about it."

"Le Bondon?"

"All five, please. I haven't decided yet which to favor."

II

At half-past eight the following morning, Wednesday, Wolfe was so furious he got some coffee in his windpipe. This was up in his bedroom, where he always eats breakfast on a tray brought by Fritz. Who got him sore was a butler—at least, the male voice on the phone was a butler's if I ever heard one. First the voice asked him to spell his name, and then, after keeping him waiting too long, told him that Mrs. Whitten did not care to speak with any newspapermen. After that double insult I was surprised he even remembered there was coffee left in his cup, and it was only natural he should swallow the wrong way.

Also we were up a stump, since if we were going to make a start at honoring Marko's draft on Wolfe's affection we certainly would have to get in touch with Mrs. Whitten or some member of the family.

It was strictly a family affair, as we had got it from the newspapers and from Marko's account of what Virgil Pompa had told him. Six months ago Mrs. Floyd Whitten had been not Mrs. Whitten but Mrs. H. R. Landy, a widow, and sole owner of AMBROSIA. You have certainly seen an AMBROSIA unless you're a hermit, and have probably eaten in one or more. The only ones I have ever patronized are AMBROSIA 19, on Grand Central Parkway near Forest Hills, Long Island; AMBROSIA 26, on Route 7 south of Danbury; and AMBROSIA 47, on Route 202 at Flemington, New Jersey. Altogether, in twelve states, either ninety-four thousand people or ninety-four million, I forget which, eat at an AMBROSIA every day.

H. R. Landy created it and built it up to AMBROSIA 109, died of overwork, and left everything to his wife. He also left her two sons and two daughters. Jerome, thirty-three, was a partner in a New York real estate firm. Mortimer, thirty-one, sort of fiddled around with radio packages and show business. And only the Internal Revenue Bureau, if anyone, knew how he was making out. Eve, twenty-seven, was Mrs. Daniel Bahr, having married the newspaper columnist whose output appeared in three times as many states as AMBROSIA had got to. Phoebe, twenty-four, had graduated from Vassar and then pitched in to help mama run AMBROSIA.

But most of the running of AMBROSIA had been up to Virgil Pompa, after Landy's death. Years ago Landy had coaxed him away from high cuisine by talking money, thereby causing him, as Marko had put it, to forfeit all claim to professional respect. But he had gained other kinds of respect and had got to be

Landy's trusted field captain and second in command. When Landy died Pompa had almost automatically taken over, but it had soon begun to get a little difficult. The widow had started to get ideas, one especially, that son Mortimer should take the wheel. However, that experiment had lasted only two months, coming to an abrupt end when Mortimer had bought eight carloads of black-market lamb which proved to have worms or something. Then for a while the widow had merely been irritating, and Pompa had decided to carry on until his seventieth birthday. It became even easier for him when Mrs. Landy married a man named Floyd Whitten, for she took her new husband on a three months' trip in South America, and when they returned to New York she was so interested in him that she went to the AMBROSIA headquarters in the Empire State Building only one or two mornings a week. Phoebe, the youngest daughter, had been on the job, but had been inclined to listen to reason—that is, to Pompa.

Suddenly, a month ago, Mrs. Whitten had told Pompa that he was old enough to retire, and that they would start immediately to train her husband to take over the direction of the business.

This dope on Floyd Whitten is partly from the papers, but mostly from Pompa via Marko. For a year before Landy's death Whitten had been in charge of public relations for AMBROSIA, and had kept on after Landy died, but when he married the boss, and came back from the long trip with his bride, he didn't resume at the office. Either he wanted to spend his time with her, or she wanted to spend hers with him, or both. Whitten (this from Pompa) was a smoothie who knew how to work his tongue. He was too selfish and conceited to get married, though he had long enjoyed intimate relations with a Miss Julie Alving, a woman about his age who earned her living by buying toys for Meadow's department store. It appeared that the facts about Whitten which had outraged Pompa most were, first, he had married a woman a dozen years his senior, second, he had coolly and completely discarded Julie Alving when he married his boss, and third, he had kept extra shirts in his office at AMBROSIA so he could change every day after lunch. It was acknowledged and established that any draft by Whitten on Pompa's affection would have been returned with the notation *Insufficient Funds*.

So the situation had stood the evening of Monday, July fifth—twenty-four hours before Marko had appealed to Wolfe to save Pompa from a murder conviction. That Monday had of course been a holiday, but Mrs. Whitten, proceeding with characteristic slapdash energy to get her husband trained for top man in AMBROSIA, had arranged a meeting for eight-thirty that evening at her house in the East Seventies between Fifth and Madison. She and Whitten would drive in from their country place near Katonah, which had been named AMBROSIA 1000 by the late Mr. Landy, though the public was neither admitted nor fed there, and Pompa would join them for a training session.

Pompa had done so, arriving at the Landy (then nominally Whitten) town house in a taxi precisely at half-past eight, and having with him a large leather case full of knives, forks, and spoons, but mostly knives. One of the tabloids had had a grand time with that prop, presenting the statistics that the case had contained a total of 126 knives, with blades all the way from 1½ inches in length to 28 inches, and speculating on the probability of any man being so thorough and comprehensive in providing himself with a murder weapon. The reason for Pompa's toting the leather case was silly but simple. Mrs. Whitten, having decided that her husband was to be It in AMBROSIA, had made a list of over a hundred items to be embraced in his training, and they had reached Item 43, which was Buying of Cutlery.

Pompa pushed the bell button several times without result. That didn't surprise him, since he knew that the servants were at AMBROSIA 1000 for the summer, and there was no telling how much the heavy holiday traffic might delay Mr. and Mrs. Whitten, driving in from the country. He had waited on the stoop only a few minutes when they drove up, in a long low special body job with Whitten at the wheel, parked at the curb, and joined him. Whitten used a key on the door and they entered.

The house, which Pompa knew well, had four stories. The first floor had a reception hall, a large living room to the right, and a dining room in the rear. The stairs were at the left of the reception hall. The trio had mounted directly to the second floor, where the front room had been used by H. R. Landy as an office-at-home and was now similarly used by Mrs. Whitten. They got down to business at once, and Pompa opened the leather case and took knives out. Whitten graciously pretended to be interested, though his real attitude was that it was foolish to waste time on Item 43, since cutlery buying was a minor detail which should be left to a subordinate. But Mrs. Whitten was quite serious about it, and therefore they stuck for nearly an hour to the contents of the leather case before Whitten managed to get onto the subject he was really hot about: unit managers.

There were four managers whom Whitten wanted to fire immediately, and one that he wanted to trans-

fer to headquarters in New York. Within five minutes
he had got sarcastic and personal, and Pompa was
yelling at the top of his voice. Pompa, according to
Marko, had always been a yeller and always would be.
When Mrs. Whitten, intervening, lined up on her husband's side, it was too much. Pompa yelled that he
was done, finished, and through for good, and tramped
out and down the stairs. Mrs. Whitten came after him,
caught him in the reception hall, and pulled him into
the living room. She appealed to him, but he stood
pat. She made him sit down, and practically sat on
him, and insisted. She was keenly aware, she said,
that no one, not even her Floyd, was capable of di-
recting successfully the complex and far-flung AMBRO-
SIA enterprise without long and thorough preparation.
Her attempt to put her son Mortimer in charge had
taught her a lesson. One more year was all she asked
of Pompa. She knew he owed no loyalty to her, and
certainly not to Floyd, but what about the dead H. R.
Landy and AMBROSIA itself? Would he desert the magnificent structure he had helped to build? As for the
immediate point at issue, she would promise that
Floyd should have no authority regarding unit managers for at least six months. Pompa, weakening,
stated that Floyd was not even to mention managers.
Mrs. Whitten agreed, kissed Pompa on the cheek,
took his hand, and led him out of the room and across
the reception hall to the stairs. They had been in the
living room with the door closed, by Pompa's best
guess, about half an hour.

As they started to mount the stairs they heard a
noise, a crash of something falling, from the dining
room.

Mrs. Whitten said something like "My God."
Pompa strode to the door to the dining room and

threw it open. It was dark in there, but there was enough light from the hall, through the door he had opened, to see that there were people. He stepped to the wall switch and flipped it. By then Mrs. Whitten was in the doorway, and they both stood and gaped. There were indeed people, five of them, now all on their feet: the two Landy sons, Jerome and Mortimer; the two Landy daughters, Eve and Phoebe; and the son-in-law, Eve's husband, Daniel Bahr. As for the noise that had betrayed them, there was an over-turned floor lamp.

Pompa, having supposed that these sons and daughters of AMBROSIA wealth were miles away on Independence Day weekends, continued to gape. So, for a moment, did Mrs. Whitten. Then, in a voice shaking either with anger or something else, she asked Pompa to go and wait for her in the living room. He left, closing the dining-room door behind him, and stood outside and listened.

The voices he heard were mostly those of Jerome, Eve, Daniel Bahr, and Mrs. Whitten. It was Bahr, the son-in-law—the only one, according to Pompa, not in awe of Mother—who told her what the conclave was for. They had gathered thus secretly and urgently to consider and discuss the matter of Floyd Whitten. Did the intention to train him to become the operating head of AMBROSIA mean that he would get control, and eventually ownership, of the source of the family fortune? If so, could anything be done, and what? He, Bahr, had come because Eve asked him to. For his part, he was glad that Mr. and Mrs. Whitten had unexpectedly arrived on the scene, and that an accidental noise had betrayed their presence; they had been sitting in scared silence, as darkness came, for nearly two hours, afraid even to sneak away because of the upstairs windows overlooking the street, talking only in low whispers, which was preposterous conduct for civilized adults. The way to handle such matters was open discussion, not furtive scheming. The thing to do now was to get Whitten down there with them and talk it out—or fight it out, if it had to be a fight.

The others talked some too, but Bahr, the professional word user, had more to use. Pompa had been surprised at Mrs. Whitten. He had supposed she would start slashing and mow them down, reminding them that AMBROSIA belonged exclusively to her, a fact she frequently found occasion to refer to, but apparently the shock of finding them there in privy powwow, ganging up on her Floyd, had cramped her style. She had not exactly wailed, but had come close to it, and had reproached them bitterly for ever dreaming that she could forget or ignore their right to a proper share in the proceeds of their father's work. For that a couple of them apologized. Finally Bahr took over again, insisting that they should bring Whitten down and reach a complete understanding. There were murmurs of agreement with him, and when Mrs. Whitten seemed about to vote yes too, Pompa decided it was time for him to move. He walked out the front door and went home.

That was all we had from Pompa. He wasn't there when Mrs. Whitten and her son Jerome and Daniel Bahr went upstairs together to get Whitten, and found him hunched over on the table with a knife in him from the back. It was one of the pointed slicing knives, with an eight-inch blade.

III

Wednesday morning, as I said, in Wolfe's bedroom, when he started to save old Virgil Pompa by getting Mrs. Whitten on the phone before he finished breakfast, instead of getting Mrs. Whitten he got coffee in his windpipe. He coughed explosively, gasped, and went on coughing.

"You shouldn't try to drink when you're mad," I told him. "Peristalsis is closely connected with the emotions. Anyhow, I think it was only a butler. Naturally she has brought the hired help in from the country. Do you care whether a butler has heard of you? I don't."

With the panic finally out of his windpipe, Wolfe took off his yellow silk pajama top, revealing enough hide to make shoes for four platoons, tossed it on the bed, and frowned at me.

"I have to see those people. Preferably all of them, but certainly Mrs. Whitten. Apparently they squirm if she grunts. Find out about her."

So that was what I spent the day at.

The Homicide Bureau was of course a good bet, and, deciding a phone call would be too casual, I did a few morning chores in the office and then went to 20th Street. Inspector Cramer wasn't available, but I got to Sergeant Purley Stebbins. I was handicapped because my one good piece of bait couldn't be used. It was a fair guess that Mrs. Whitten and the Landy children had given the cops a distorted view of the reason for the secret gathering in the dining room and the two-hour silent sit in the dark—possibly even a fancy lie. If so, it would have helped to be able to give Purley the lowdown on it, but I couldn't. Pompa, when first questioned by the city employees, had stated that when Mrs. Whitten had asked him to go to the living room and wait there for her, he had done so, and had left when he got tired of waiting. The damn fool hadn't wanted to admit he had eavesdropped, and now he was stuck with it. If he tried to change it, or if Wolfe and I tried to change it for him, it would merely make his eye blacker than ever and no one would believe him.

Therefore the best I could do with Purley was to tell him Wolfe had been hired to spring Pompa, and of course that went over big. He was so sure they had Pompa for good that after a couple of supercilious snorts he got bighearted and conversed a little. It seemed that the secret meeting of scions in the dining room had been to discuss a scrape Mortimer had got into—a threatened paternity suit—which mamma mustn't know about. So for me they were a bunch of barefaced liars, since Wolfe had decided to take Pompa for gospel. Purley had lots of fun kidding me, sure as he was that for once Wolfe had got roped in for a sour one. I took it, and also took all I could get on Mrs. Whitten and other details. The Homicide and DA line was that while waiting for Mrs. Whitten in the living room Pompa had got bored and, instead of just killing time, had trotted upstairs and killed Whitten, who was about to toss him out of his job.

Altogether I saw eight or nine people that day, building up an inventory on Mrs. Whitten and her offspring, and bought a drink for nobody, since there was no client's expense account. They were a couple of radio men, a realtor who had once paid Wolfe a fee, a gossip peddler, and others, naturally including my friend Lon Cohen of the *Gazette*. During the afternoon Lon was tied up on some hot item, and I got to him so late that I made it back to West 35th Street barely in time for dinner. Marko Vukcic was there when I arrived.

After a meal fully as good as the one Marko had fed us the evening before, the three of us went across the hall to the office. Wolfe got himself arranged in the chair behind his desk, the only chair on earth he really loves; Marko sat on the red leather one; and I stood and had a good stretch.

"Television?" Wolfe inquired politely.

"In the name of God," Marko protested. "Pompa will die soon, perhaps tonight."

"What of?"

"Fear, rage, mortification. He is old."

"Nonsense. He will live to get his eye back, if for nothing else." Wolfe shook his head. "As you said yesterday, Marko, you're a Boniface, not a detective. Don't crack a whip at me. What have you got, Archie?"

"No news." I pulled my chair away from my desk and sat. "Are we still swallowing Pompa whole?"

"Yes."

"Then they're all lying about what they were there for, except Daniel Bahr, Eve's husband, who merely says it was a family matter which he prefers not to discuss. They say they met to consider a jam Mortimer is in with a female by the name of—"

"No matter. Mrs. Whitten?"

"She's in on the lie, of course. Probably she clucked them into it. During Landy's life he was absolutely the rooster, and she merely came along with the flock, but when he died she took command and kept it. She is of the flock, by the flock, and for the flock, or at least she was until Whitten got his hooks in. Since her marriage she has unquestionably been for Whitten, though there has been no sign that she intended to swear off clucking—at least there wasn't until a month ago, when she installed Whitten in the big corner office that had been Landy's. Pompa never moved into it. She is fifty-four, fairly bright, watches her figure, and looks as healthy as she is."

"Have you seen her?"

"How could I? She wouldn't even talk to you on the phone."

"The son, Mortimer. Is he really in a scrape? Does he urgently need money?"

"Sure, I suppose so, like lots of other people, but this girl trouble is apparently nothing desperate, only enough of a mess so they could drag it in. About people urgently needing money, who knows? Maybe they all do. Jerome owns part of a real estate business, but he's a big spender. Mortimer could owe a million. Eve and her husband might be betting on horse races, if you want to be trite. Phoebe may want to finance a big deal in narcotics, though that would be pretty precocious at twenty-four. There are plenty—"

"Archie. Quit talking. Report."

I did so. It filled an hour and went on into the second, my display of all the little scraps I had collected, while Wolfe leaned back with his eyes closed and Marko obviously got more and more irritated. When the question period was finished too Marko exploded.

"Sacred Father above! If I prepared a meal like this my patrons would all starve to death! Pompa will die not of fear but of old age!"

Wolfe made allowances. "My friend," he said patiently, "when you are preparing a meal the cutlet or loin does not use all possible resource, cunning, resolution, and malice to evade your grasp. But a murderer does. Assuming that Mr. Pompa is innocent, as I do on your assurance, manifestly one of those six people is behind a shield that cannot be removed by a finger's flick. They may even be in concert, if one of them went upstairs and dealt with Mr. Whitten while Mrs. Whitten and Mr. Pompa were in the living room. But before I can move I must start." Wolfe looked at the clock on the wall, which said ten past ten, and then at me. "Archie."

"Yes, sir."

"Get them down here. As many of them as possible."

"Yeah. During the week?"

"Tonight. Now."

I gawked at him. "You don't mean it."

"The devil I don't." He was positively serious. "You probably can't do it, but you can try. Confound it, look at Marko! At least you can bring the younger daughter. A woman that age likes to be with you no matter where you go, heaven knows why."

"It's my glass eye and wooden leg." I stood up. "This is Wednesday. Hold your breath until Saturday." I crossed to the door, and asked over my shoulder, "Have you any suggestions?"

"None. The circumstances may offer one."

IV

Since there would be no parking problem in the East Seventies at that hour, I decided to take my own wheels and went around the corner to the garage for the car.

On the way uptown I went over it. I was quite aware that Wolfe didn't really expect me to deliver, not even Phoebe. He merely wanted to get Marko off his neck, and sending me out to pass a miracle was his first and most natural notion, and also the least trouble for him. He knew it would make me sore, so the first thing I decided was not to be sore. When, stopping for a light on Fifth Avenue in the Forties, I caught myself muttering, "The fat lazy bum," I saw that wasn't working very good and took a fresh hold.

I parked a few yards west of the house I wanted to get into, on the same side of the street, just back of a dark gray sedan with an MD plate alongside the license. Sitting there with my eyes on the house entrance, which was the sort of granite portal to be expected in that upper-bracket neighborhood, I tried going over it again. I could get the door to open just by pushing the bell button. I could get inside by the momentum of 180 pounds. There were even simple stratagems that would probably get me to Mrs. Whitten. But what about from there on? With the house right there in front of me I got ambitious. It would be nice to make a delivery that Wolfe didn't expect. The notion of playing it straight, saying that we had been engaged by Pompa and would like to have a conversation with the family, had been rejected before I had got to 42nd Street. I had other notions, some risky, some screwy, and some clever, but nothing that seemed to fit all the requirements. When I looked at my wrist watch and saw 10:40 I decided I had better settle for one and shoot it, did so, and climbed out to the sidewalk. As I swung the car door shut, I saw a man emerging from the entrance I was bound for. The light wasn't very bright there, but there was plenty to see that it wasn't either of the sons or the son-in-law. He was past middle age, and he was carrying the kind of black case that means doctor anywhere. He crossed the sidewalk to the gray sedan with an MD plate on it, got in, and rolled away. Naturally, with my training and habits, I automatically noted the license number and filed it.

I walked to the portal, entered the vestibule, and pushed the button. In a moment the door opened enough to show me a baldheaded guy in conventional black, with a big pointed nose, and to show me to him.

"My name is Archie Goodwin," I informed him, "and I would like to see Mrs. Whitten."

He said authoritatively, "No newspapermen are being admitted," and started to close the door. My foot stopped it after a couple of inches.

"You have newspapermen on the brain," I told him courteously but firmly. "I happen to be a detective." I got my card case from my pocket. "Like this." I pulled my license card, with photograph and thumbprint, from under the cellophane and handed it to him, and he inspected it.

"This does not indicate," he asserted, "that you are a member of the police force."

"I didn't say I was. I merely—"

"What's the trouble, Borly?" a voice came from behind him. He turned, and the pressure of my foot made the door swing in more. Since an open door is universally regarded as an invitation to enter, I crossed the threshold.

"There's no trouble, Mr. Landy," I said cheerfully. "The butler was just doing his duty." As I spoke two other men came in sight from a door to the right, which made it four to one. I was going on. "My name's Goodwin, and I work for Nero Wolfe, and I want to see Mrs. Whitten."

"The hell you do. On out." With a gesture he indicated the door he wished me to use. "I said out!"

He took a step toward me. I was mildly confused

because I hadn't expected to have to deal with a whole quartet immediately on entering. Of course it was no trick to spot them, from their pictures in the papers and descriptions. The one outing me, which he might possibly have done since he was a little bigger, up to heavyweight specifications, with a big red face having eyes too far apart, was Mortimer. The one with dark hair slicked back, wirier and smaller and smarter looking, was his elder brother Jerome. The middle-sized one, who looked like a washed-out high school teacher, was their brother-in-law, the famous columnist who was more widespread than AMBROSIA, Daniel Bahr.

"You can," I admitted, "put me out, but if you wait half a minute you can still put me out. I have come to see Mrs. Whitten on behalf of Miss Julie Alving. It would be only fair to let Mrs. Whitten herself decide whether she wants to see someone who wishes to speak for Miss Alving. If you—"

"Beat it." He took another step. "You're damn right we can put you out—"

"Take it easy, Mort." Jerome was approaching, in no haste or alarm. He saw the license card in the butler's hand, took it and glanced at it, and handed it to me. "My mother's upstairs asleep. I'm Jerome Landy. Tell me what you want to say for Miss Alving and I'll see that it gets attention."

"She's asleep?"

"Yes."

"Who's sick?"

"Sick?"

"Yeah. Ill."

"I don't know. Not me. Why?"

"I just saw a doctor leave here carrying his case, and of course if he gave her sleeping pills and then stopped for a chat with you, naturally she would be asleep now. It's the way a detective's mind works, that's all." I grinned at him. "Unless she's not the patient. One of your sisters maybe? Anyhow, I have nothing to say for Miss Alving except direct to Mrs. Whitten. I don't know whether she would agree that it's urgent and strictly personal, and there's no way of deciding but to ask her. By tomorrow it might be too late. I don't know about that either."

"Ask him," suggested Daniel Bahr, who had joined us, "whether it's a request for money. If it is an attempt at a shakedown there is only one possible answer."

"If that was it," I said, "our blackmail department would be handling it, and I've been promoted from that. That's as far as I can go except to Mrs. Whitten."

"Wait here," Jerome instructed me, and made for the stairs.

I stood in quiet dignity, but allowed my eyes to move. This, of course, was the reception hall, with the stairs at the left, the door to the living room on the right, and at the far end the door to the dining room, where the secret meeting of sons and daughters had been held. The hall was large and high-ceilinged and not overfurnished, except maybe a pink marble thing against the wall beyond the living-room door. It had a bare look because there was nothing but a couple of straw mats on the floor, but since it was July that was understandable. The only action while Jerome was gone was Mortimer's dismissing the butler, who disappeared through the door to the dining room.

It wasn't too long before Jerome came halfway down the stairs and called to me.

"Up here, Goodwin."

I mounted to join him. On the landing above he turned to face me.

"You'll keep it brief. I'm telling you. Is that understood?"

"Sure."

"My mother's in bed but not asleep. The doctor didn't give her sleeping pills because she doesn't need them. Her heart isn't as good as it might be, and what happened here night before last, and these two days —I tried to persuade her not to see you, but she takes a lot of persuading. You'll make it brief?"

"Sure."

I followed him up to the third floor, which seemed a bad location for a woman with a weak heart, and into a room at the front. Inside I halted. Within range there was not one woman, but three. The one standing over by the bed, dark and small like Jerome, was Eve. The one who had been doing something at a bureau and turned as we entered was Phoebe, the child who, according to my day's collection of scraps, most resembled her father. My quick glance at her gave me the impression that Father could have asked for no nicer compliment. Jerome was pronouncing my name, and I advanced to the bedside. As I did so there were steps to my rear and I swiveled my neck enough to get a glimpse of Mortimer and Daniel Bahr entering. That made it complete—all the six that Wolfe wanted to see!

But not for long. A voice of authority came from the bed.

"You children get out!"

"But mother—"

They all protested. From the way she insisted, not with any vehemence, it was obvious that she took obedience for granted, and she got it, though for a moment I thought Phoebe, who was said to resemble her father, might stick it. But she too went, the last one out, and closed the door after her as instructed.

"Well?" Mrs. Whitten demanded. She took in a long breath, with a long loud sigh. "What about Miss Alving?"

She was lying flat on her back with a thin blue silk coverlet nearly up to her throat, and against the blue pillow her face was so pale that I might not have recognized her from the pictures and descriptions. That made her look older, of course, and then her hair was in no condition for public display. But the snap and fire were in her eyes, as specified, and the firm pointed chin was even exaggerated at that angle.

"What about her?" she repeated impatiently.

"Excuse me," I apologized. "I was wondering if I should bother you after all—right now. You look sick."

"I'm not sick. It's only—my heart." She took a long sighing breath. "What would you expect? What about Miss Alving?"

I could and would have done better if my mind had been on it, but it wasn't. I couldn't even remember which tack I had decided to take, because an interesting idea had not only entered my head but evicted all the previous tenants. But I couldn't just turn on my heel and blow, so I spoke.

"I don't want to be crude, Mrs. Whitten, but you understand that while you have your personal situation and problems, other people have theirs. At least you will grant that the death of Floyd Whitten means more to Miss Alving than it does to people who never knew him, though they're all reading about it and talking about it. The idea was for Nero Wolfe to have a little talk with you regarding certain aspects of the situation which are of special interest to Miss Alving."

"I owe Miss Alving nothing." Mrs. Whitten had raised her head from the pillow, aiming her eyes at me, but now she let it fall back, and again she sighed, taking in all the air she could get. "It is no secret that my husband knew her once, but their—it was ended when he got married. That is no secret either."

"I know that," I agreed. "But I couldn't discuss things even if I knew about them. I'm just a messenger boy. My job was to arrange for Mr. Wolfe to talk with you, and it looks as if I'll have to pass it up for now, since he never leaves his house to see anyone on business, and you can't very well be expected to leave yours if your doctor has put you to bed." I grinned down at her. "That's why I apologized for bothering you. Maybe tomorrow or next day?" I backed away. "I'll phone you, or Mr. Wolfe will."

Her head had come up again. "You're going to tell me," she said in a tone that could not have been called a cluck, "exactly why Miss Alving sent you here to annoy me."

"I can't," I told her from the door. "Because I don't know. And I promised your son I'd make it brief." I turned the knob and pulled. "You'll be hearing from us."

Two daughters and a son were out on the landing. "Okay," I told them cheerfully, got by, and started down. Bahr and Mortimer were in the reception hall, and I nodded as I breezed past, opened the door for myself, and was out.

Since what I wanted was the nearest phone booth, I turned left, toward Madison, and one block down, at the corner, entered a drug store.

Routine would have been to call Wolfe and get his opinion of my interesting idea, but he had sicked me onto them with nothing to go by but his snooty remark that circumstances might offer suggestions, so I went right past him. I could have got what I wanted from 20th Street, but if I got a break and my hunch grew feathers I didn't want the Homicide boys in on it, so the number I dialed was that of the *Gazette* office. Lon Cohen was always there until midnight, so I soon had him.

"I'm looking," I told him, "for a good doctor to pierce my ears for earrings, and I think I've found one. Call me at this number"—I gave it to him—"and tell me who New York license UMX four three three one seven belongs to."

He had me repeat it, which shouldn't have been necessary with a veteran newspaperman. I hung up and did my waiting outside the booth, since the temperature inside was well over a hundred. The phone rang in five minutes, exactly par for that routine item of research, and a voice—not Lon's, for he was a busy man at that time of night—gave me a name and address: Frederick M. Cutler, M.D., with an office on East 65th and a residence on Park Avenue.

It was ten blocks away, so I went for the car and drove it, parked on the avenue a polite distance from the canopy with the number on it, and went in. The lobby was all it should have been in that locality, and the night man took exactly the right attitude toward a complete stranger. On my way I had decided what would be exactly the right attitude for me.

"Dr. Frederick M. Cutler," I said. "Please phone up."

"Name?"

"Tell him a private detective named Goodwin has an important question to ask him about the patient he was visiting forty minutes ago."

I thought that would do. If that got me to him my

hunch would already have an attractive fuzz on its bare pink skin. So when, after finishing at the phone, he crossed to the elevator with me and told his colleague I was to be conveyed to 12C, my heart had accelerated a good ten per cent.

At 12C I was admitted by the man I had seen leaving the Whitten house with his black case. Here, with a better view of him, I could note such details as the gray in his hair, his impatient gray-blue eyes, and the sag at the corners of his wide full mouth. Also I could see, through an arch, men and women at a couple of card tables in the large room beyond.

"Come this way, please," my victim said gruffly, and I followed him down a hall and through a door. This was a small room, its walls solid with books, and a couch, a desk, and three chairs, leaving no space at all. He closed the door, confronted me, and was even gruffer.

"What do you want?"

The poor guy had already given me at least half of what I wanted, but of course he would have had to be very nifty on the draw not to.

"My name," I said, "is Archie Goodwin, and I work for Nero Wolfe."

"So that's who you are. What do you want?"

"I was sent to see Mrs. Floyd Whitten, and while I was parking my car in front I saw you leaving her house. Naturally I recognized you, since you are pretty well known." I thought he might as well have a lump of sugar. "I went in and had a little talk with Mrs. Whitten up in her bedroom. Her son said, and she said, that the trouble was her heart. But then how come? There is a widespread opinion that she is in splendid health and always has been. At her age she plays tennis. She walks up two flights to her bedroom.

People who know her admire her healthy complexion.
But when I saw her, there in bed, she was as pale as a
corpse, in fact she was pale *like* a corpse, and she kept
taking long sighing breaths. I'm not a doctor, but I
happen to know that those two symptoms—that kind
of pallor and that kind of breathing—go with a consid-
erable loss of blood, say over a pint. She didn't have a
cardiac hemorrhage, did she?"

Cutler's jaw was working. "The condition of my
patient is none of your business. But Mrs. Whitten
has had an extremely severe shock."

"Yeah, I know she has. But the business I'm in, I
have seen quite a few people under the shock of the
sudden death of someone they loved, and I've seen a
slew of reactions, and this one is brand new. The pallor possibly, but combined with those long frequent
sighs?" I shook my head. "I will not settle for that.
Besides, why did you let me come up after the kind of
message I sent, if it's just shock? Why did you let me
in and herd me back here so private? At this point I
think you ought to either toss me out or invite me to
sit down."

He did neither. He glared.

"Lookit," I said, perfectly friendly. "Do some supposing. Suppose you were called there and found her
with a wound and a lot of blood gone. You did what
was needed, and when she asked you to keep it quiet
you decided to humor her and ignore your legal obligation to make a report to the authorities in such
cases. Ordinarily that would be nothing for a special
broadcast; doctors do it every day. But this is far from
ordinary. Her husband was murdered, stabbed to
death. A man named Pompa has been charged with it,
but he's not convicted yet. Suppose one of the five
people hid in the dining room killed Whitten? They

could have, easily, while Pompa and Mrs. Whitten
were in the living room—a whole half-hour. Those five
people are in Mrs. Whitten's house with her now, and
two of them live there. Suppose the motive for killing
Whitten is good for her too, and one of them tried it,
and maybe tonight or tomorrow makes another try
and this time it works? How would you feel about
clamming up on the first try? How would others feel
when it came out, as it would?"

"You're crazy," Cutler growled. "They're her sons
and daughters!"

"Oh, for God's sake," I growled back at him. "And
you a doctor who sees inside people? The parents who
have been killed by sons and daughters would fill a
hundred cemeteries. I'm not crazy, but I'm good and
scared. I guess I scare easier than you. I say that
woman has lost blood, and you're not denying it, so
one of two things has to happen. Either you give me
the lowdown confidentially, and it will have to sound
right, or I suggest to the cops that they send a doctor
to have a look at her. Then if my supposes all come
true I won't have to feel that I helped to kill her. How
you will feel is your affair."

"The police have no right to invade a citizen's pri-
vacy in that manner."

"You'd be surprised. In a house where a murder
was committed, and she was there and so were they?"

"Your suppositions are contrary to the facts."

"Fine. That's what I'm after, the facts. Let me
have a look at them. If they appeal to us, Mr. Wolfe
and I can ignore obligations as easy as you."

He sat down, rested his elbows on the arms of the
chair with his hands dangling, and thoroughly inspected a corner of a rug. I inspected him. He stood

up again, said, "I'll be back shortly," and started for the door.

"Hold it," I snapped. "This is your place and I can't keep you from going to another room to phone, but if you do, any facts you furnish will need a lot of checking. It all comes down to which you like better, giving it to me straight or having a police doctor go over your patient."

"I ought to kick you the hell out of here," he said grimly.

I shook my head. "Not now. If you had taken that attitude when that message was phoned up to you I would have had to think again, but now it's too late." I gestured at the desk. "Use that phone, if all you want is to tell Mrs. Whitten that a skunk named Goodwin has got you by the tail and you've got to break your promise to keep it quiet." I took a step and held his eye with mine. "You see, brother, when I said I was scared I meant it. Sons and daughters phooey. If Pompa is innocent, and he is, there's a murderer in that house, and an animal that has killed can kill again, and often does. What is going on there right now? I'd like to know, and I'm getting tired of talking to you. And what's more, something's biting you too or you wouldn't have let me up here."

Cutler went and sat down again, and I sat on the edge of the couch, facing him. I waited.

"It couldn't be," he declared.

"What couldn't be?"

"Something biting me."

"Something bit Mrs. Whitten. Or was it a bite or a bullet or what?"

"It was a cut." His voice was weary and precise, not gruff at all. "Her son Jerome phoned me at a quarter to ten, and I went at once. She was upstairs on the bed and things were bloody. They had towels against her, pressing the wound together. There was a cut on her left side, five inches long and deep enough to expose the eighth rib, and a shallow cut on her left arm above the elbow, two inches long. The cuts had been made with a sharp blade. Twelve sutures were required in the side wound, and four in the arm. The loss of blood had been substantial, but not serious enough to call for more than iron and liver, which I prescribed. That was all. I left."

"How did she get cut?"

"I was proceeding to tell you. She said she had gone in the late afternoon to a conference in her business office, made urgent by the death of her husband and the arrest of Pompa. It had lasted longer than expected. Riding back uptown, she had dismissed her chauffeur, sent him home in a taxi, and had driven herself around the park for a while. Then she drove to her house. As she got out of her car someone seized her from behind, and she thought she was being kidnaped. She gouged with her elbows and kicked, and suddenly her assailant released her and darted away. She crossed the sidewalk to her door, rang, and was admitted by Borly, the butler. Only after she was inside did she learn that she had been stabbed, or cut. The sons and daughters were there, and they phoned me and got her upstairs. They also, directed by her, cleaned up; indoors and out. The butler washed the sidewalk with a hose. He was doing that when I arrived. Mrs. Whitten explained to me that the haste in cleaning up was on account of her desire to have no hullabaloo, as she put it. Under the circumstances the episode would naturally have been greatly—uh, magnified. She asked me to do her the favor of exercising professional discretion, and I saw no sufficient reason to refuse. I shall explain to her that your threat to have a police doctor see her left me no choice."

He turned up his palms. "Those are the facts."

I nodded. "As you got them. Who was it that jumped her?"

"She doesn't know."

"Man or woman?"

"She doesn't know. She was attacked from behind, and it was after dark. When her assailant dashed off, by the time she got straightened and turned he—or she—was the other side of a parked car. Anyway, she was frightened, and her concern was safety."

"She didn't see him before he jumped her? As she drove up?"

"No. He could have been concealed behind the parked car."

"Were there no passers-by?"

"None. No one appeared."

"Did she scream?"

"I didn't ask her." He was getting irritated. "I didn't subject her to an inquisition, you know. She had been hurt and needed attention, and I gave it to her."

"Sure." I stood up. "I won't say much obliged because I squeezed it out. I accept your facts—that is, what you were told—but I ought to warn you that you may get a phone call from Nero Wolfe. I can find my way out."

He stood up. "I think you used the word 'confidential.' May I tell Mrs. Whitten that she need not expect a visit from a police doctor?"

"I'll do my best. I mean it. But if I were you I wouldn't give her any more quick promises. They're apt not to stick."

I reached for the doorknob, but he was ahead of me and opened it. He took me back down the hall and let me out, and even told me good night. The elevator man kept slanted eyes on me, evidently having been told of the vulgar message I had sent up to a tenant, so I told him that his starting lever needed oil, which it did. Outside I climbed in the car and rolled downtown a little faster than I was supposed to. The clock on the dash said ten minutes to midnight.

When I'm not in the house, especially at night, the front door is always chain bolted, so I had to ring for Fritz to let me in. I went along with him to the kitchen, got a glass and a pitcher of milk, took them to the office, and announced, "Home again, and I brought no company. But I've got a tool I think you can pry Pompa loose with, if you want to play it that way. I need some milk on my stomach. My nerves are doubling in brass."

"What is it?" Marko demanded, out of his chair at me. "What did you—"

"Let him alone," Wolfe muttered, "until he has swallowed something. He's hungry."

V

"If you don't tell the police about this at once, I will," Marko said emphatically. He hit the chair arm with his fist. "This is magnificent! It is a masterpiece of wit!"

I had finished my report, along with the pitcher of milk, and Wolfe had asked questions, such as whether I had seen any bloodstains, inside or out, which the cleaners had overlooked. I hadn't. Wolfe was leaning back in his chair with his eyes closed, and Marko was pacing back and forth. I was smirking, but not visibly.

"They must release him at once!" Marko exclaimed. "Tell them now! Phone! If you don't—"

"Shut up," Wolfe said rudely.

"He's using his brain," I informed Marko, "and you're breaking the rules. Yell at me if you want to, but not at him. It's not as simple as it looks. If we pass it to the cops it's out of our hands, and if they're stubborn and still like the idea of Pompa where are we? We couldn't get through to that bunch again with anything less than a Sherman tank. If we don't tell the cops but keep it for our private use, and we monkey around until whoever used a knife on Mrs. Whitten uses it again only more to the point, the immediate question would be how high the judge would set our bail."

"Including me?" Marko demanded.

"Certainly including you. You especially, because you started the conspiracy to spring Pompa."

Marko stopped pacing to frown at me. "But you make it impossible. We can't tell the police, and we can't not tell the police. Is this what I called a masterpiece?"

"Sure, and you were right. It was so slick that I'm going to ask for a raise. Because there's a loophole, namely we don't have to monkey around. We can keep going the way I started. We've got a club to use on Mrs. Whitten, which means all of them, and if she hadn't just been sliced and had her side sewed up we could phone her that we want her down here within the hour, along with the family. As it is, I guess that's out. The alternative is for Mr. Wolfe and me to get in the car, which is out at the curb, and go there—now."

I ignored a little grunt from Wolfe's direction.

"It has been years," I told Marko, "since I tried to get him to break his rule never to go anywhere outside this house on business, and I wouldn't waste breath on it now. But this has nothing to do with business. You're not a client, and Pompa isn't, and he has told you that he wouldn't take your money. This is for love, a favor to an old friend, which makes it entirely different. No question of rule-breaking is involved."

Marko was gazing at me. "You mean go to Mrs. Whitten's home?"

"Certainly. Why not?"

"Would they let you in?"

"You're damn right they would, if that doctor has phoned her, and it's ten to one he did."

"Would it accomplish anything?"

"The least it would accomplish would be that there wouldn't be a second murder as long as we were there. Beyond that—circumstances might offer suggestions. I might add, not being a candidate for president, that when I went there alone it accomplished a little something."

Marko wheeled to Wolfe with his arms extended. "Nero, you must go! At once! You must!"

Wolfe's eyes came half open, slowly. "Pfui," he said scornfully.

"But it is the only thing! Let me tell you what Archie—"

"I heard him." The open eyes saw an unfinished glass of beer, and he picked it up and drank. He looked at me. "There was a flaw. You assume that if we withhold this information from the police, and Mrs. Whitten gets killed, we'll be in a pickle. Why? Technically it is not murder evidence; it has no necessary connection with a committed crime. Legally we are clear. Morally we are also clear. What if we accept and credit Mrs. Whitten's explanation as she gives it?

Then there is no menace to her from the members of her family."

"You mean you buy it?" I demanded. "That she couldn't even tell whether it was a man or a woman?"

"Why not?"

I got up, threw up my hands, and sat down again.

"But this is not logical," Marko protested earnestly. "Your questions indicated that you thought she had lied to the doctor. I don't see why—"

"Nuts," I said in disgust. "He knows damn well she lied. If he liked to bet he would give you odds that it was one of the family that cut her up, either in the house or out, and she knows who it was and so do the rest of them. I know him better than you do, Marko. If he did leave his damn house and ride at night through the dangerous streets, when he got there he would have to work like a dog, put all he's got into it, to nail the one that has it coming. If instead of that he goes to bed and sleeps well, something may happen to simplify matters. That's all there is to it."

"Is that true, Nero?" Marko demanded.

"It contains truth," Wolfe conceded big-heartedly. "So does this. Patently Mrs. Whitten is in danger. Anyone who cuts a five-inch gash in the territory of the eighth rib may be presumed to have maleficent intentions, and probably pertinacity to boot. But though Archie is normally humane, his exasperation does not come from a benevolent passion to prevent further injury to Mrs. Whitten. She is much too old for him to feel that way. It comes from his childish resentment that his coup, which was unquestionably brilliant, will not be immediately followed up as he would like it to be. That is understandable, but I see no reason—"

The doorbell rang. I got up and went for it. I might

have left it to Fritz, but I was glad of an excuse to walk out on Wolfe's objectionable remarks. The panel in our entrance door is one-way glass, permitting us to see out but not the outsider to see in, and on my way down the hall I flipped the switch for the stoop light to get a look.

One glance was enough, but I took a step for another one before turning, marching back to the office, and telling Wolfe, "You may remember that you instructed me to get six people down here—as many of them as possible, you said. They're here. Out on the stoop. Shall I tell them you're sleepy?"

"All of them?"

"Yes, sir."

Wolfe threw his head back and laughed. He did that about once a year. When it had tapered off to a chuckle he spoke.

"Marko, will you leave by way of the front room? Through that door. Your presence might embarrass them. Bring them in, Archie."

I went back out, pulled the door wide open, and greeted them.

"Hello there! Come on in."

"You goddam rat," Mortimer snarled at me through his teeth.

VI

The two sons were supporting their mother, one on either side, and continued to do so along the hall and on into the office. She was wearing a tan summer outfit, dotted with brown, which I would have assumed to be silk if I had not heard tell that in certain shops you can part with three centuries for a little number in

rayon. Eve was in white, with yellow buttons, and
Phoebe was in what I would call calico, two shades of
blue. My impulse to smile at her of course had to be
choked.

Thinking it might prevent an outburst, or at least
postpone it, I formally pronounced their names for
Wolfe and then saw that their chairs were arranged
the way he liked it when we had a crowd, so that he
wouldn't have to work his neck too much to take them
all in. Jerome and Mortimer, declining my offer of the
big couch for Mom, got her comfortable in the red
leather chair, but it was Phoebe who took the chair
next to her. Mortimer stayed on his feet. The others
sat.

Wolfe's eyes swept the arc. "You all look mad," he
said inoffensively.

"If you think that's witty," Eve snapped.

"Not at all," he assured her. "I was merely ac-
knowledging an atmosphere." His eyes moved to Mrs.
Whitten. "Do you want me to talk, madam? You came
here, and you might like to tell me why."

"Your lousy punk," Mortimer blurted, "might like
to step outside and ask me why!"

"Mortimer!" Mrs. Whitten turned to him. "Sit
down."

He hesitated, opened his trap and shut it again,
moved, and sat, next to Phoebe. A fine brother she
picked.

"You will please remember," Mrs. Whitten told the
flock, "that I am to do the talking. I wanted to come
alone, but you talked me out of it, and now you will
please keep silent. Including you, Dan," she added to
the son-in-law. She returned to Wolfe. "I was getting
my breath. The exertion was—not too much, but

enough." She was still using sighs to get oxygen, and she was even paler than when I had seen her in bed.

"I can wait," Wolfe said placidly. "Would you like some brandy?"

"No, thank you." She breathed long and deep. "I don't take alcohol, even as medicine, though all my children do. Their father permitted it. I apologized for my son calling your associate, Mr. Goodwin, a lousy punk. Do you wish an apology from him?"

"Certainly not. He wouldn't mean it."

"I suppose not. Do you share Mr. Goodwin's opinions?"

"Often. Not always, heaven knows."

"He told Dr. Cutler that Virgil Pompa did not kill my husband, that he is innocent. Do you believe that too?"

"Yes."

"Why?"

Wolfe regarded her. "It seems to me," he suggested, "that you're going a long way round, and it's an hour past midnight, you need rest and quiet, and I have myself a great many questions to ask—all of you. What you most urgently want to know is whether I intend to tell the police about the assault that was made on you, and if not, what do I intend. That's right, isn't it?"

"It isn't only a matter of intention," Daniel Bahr said like a lecturer. "It may well be asked, by what right do you—"

"Dan, what did I tell you?" came at him from his mother-in-law.

"Hold it, chum," Mortimer growled. "We're just tassels."

"Goodness knows," Mrs. Whitten told Wolfe, "I didn't get up and dress and come down here just to have an argument. My children all love to argue, just like their father, but I don't. About my being assaulted, it was silly for me to ask my doctor not to report it, but I thought I simply couldn't stand more talks with policemen." She took a long breath. "That would have been better than this, but how could I know an extremely intelligent young man was going to come to see me on behalf of Miss Alving? He said he didn't know why she sent him, but that you did. What does she want—money? I don't owe her anything. Then he told my doctor that Virgil Pompa is innocent. Why did he tell my doctor that? Maybe he can prove Pompa is innocent—I don't know, maybe he can. If he can, that police inspector is the man to tell, not my doctor. So I thought there were several things you might tell me about."

"We agreed with her," Jerome said quietly.

"I see." Wolfe pursed his lips. His eyes took them in and settled on Mrs. Whitten. "Three things, apparently. First, Miss Alving. That is a private matter and should be tête-à-tête, so we'll postpone it. Second, the innocence of Mr. Pompa. My reasons for assuming it would convince neither the police nor you, so we won't waste time on them. Third, the assault on you with a knife. We might get somewhere discussing that."

"One thing I didn't tell Dr. Cutler," Mrs. Whitten offered. "I didn't notice it until after he had gone. My bag was stolen. The person who stabbed me must have taken it and run with it."

"Good heavens." Wolfe's eyes widened at her. "You're only making it worse, and it was bad enough already. It was a mistake to say you didn't know whether it was a man or a woman, but this is pure poppycock. A bag snatcher who carries a naked knife and uses it on your torso as he snatches? Bah!"

"She probably dropped it," Eve explained.

"And no one noticed its absence for an hour?" Wolfe shook his head. "No, this makes it worse. I offer an alternative. Either you, all of you, will discuss with me what happened up there Monday evening, and give me responsive answers to questions, or I put a case to Inspector Cramer."

"What case?" Bahr demanded.

"I'll give Mr. Cramer both the facts and my inferences. I'll tell him of Mrs. Whitten's injuries, and why her explanation of them is unacceptable. I'll say that the use of a deadly weapon on her, soon after the fatal use of a similar weapon on her husband, is highly suggestive and demands the fullest inquiry; that if the same person made both attacks, which is at least a permissible conjecture, it could not have been Mr. Pompa, since he is locked up; that if the same person made both attacks it must have been one of you five here present, since only you and Mr. Pompa had an opportunity to kill Mr. Whitten; that—"

"Why, you bastard!" Mortimer blurted.

"Keep quiet, Mort," Phoebe muttered at him.

"—that," Wolfe continued, "this conjecture gets strong support from Mrs. Whitten's untenable explanation of her injuries." Wolfe upturned a palm. "That's the kernel of it." He spoke to Mrs. Whitten. "Why would you make up a story, good or bad? To conceal the identity of your assailant. Why would you want to protect one who had used a deadly weapon on you? Because it was one of these five people, a member of your family. But it must have been one of these five people who, if Mr. Pompa is innocent, killed Mr. Whitten. It fits neatly. It deserves inquiry; I propose to inquire; and if you won't let me, then it will have to be the police."

"This was inherent in the situation," Bahr announced, as if that took the sting out of it.

"You're accusing one of us of murder," Jerome Landy told Wolfe.

"Not one, Mr. Landy. All of you. I'm not prepared yet to particularize."

"That's serious. Very serious."

"It is indeed."

"If you expect us to answer questions we have a right to have a lawyer present."

"No. You have no right at all, except to get up and leave. I am not speaking for the people of the State of New York; I am merely a private detective who has you cornered. There are two ways out, and you are free to choose. But before you do so it is only fair to warn you that I have concealed weapons. I'll show you one. I do not surmise that all of you lied to the police; I know it. You said that your clandestine meeting was for a discussion of a difficulty your brother Mortimer had encountered."

"It was," Jerome asserted.

"No, it wasn't. Mr. Bahr told Mrs. Whitten that you had gathered to consider the problem posed by her new husband. What was indicated for the future by putting him at the head of the family business? Was he to be permitted to take it over and own it? If so, what about the Landy children? Mrs. Whitten, shocked by this concerted onset, did not counterattack as might have been expected. She did not even remind you that the business belonged to her. She reproached you for assuming that she was capable of violating your rights as your father's children. During the talk Mr. Bahr twice suggested that the proper course was to have Mr. Whitten join you, and have it out. The second time he made the suggestion it was approved by all of you, including the one who knew it was futile because Mr. Whitten was dead. So, as I say, you all lied to the police."

"I didn't," Bahr declared. "I only said it was a family matter which I could not discuss."

"You see?" Wolfe snapped at them. "Thank you, Mr. Bahr. That might not be corroboration for a jury, but it is for me. Now." He aimed his eyes at Eve. "I'll start with you, Mrs. Bahr. There's no point in sequestering you, since there has been ample time to arrange for concord. During the time you five were in the dining room Monday evening, who left the room and when?"

VII

But Mrs. Whitten delayed the question period another ten minutes by entering a demurrer. She had a point all right, but it seemed foolish for her to press it then. Of course it was obvious that one of two things was true: either Pompa had made a sucker of Marko, or Wolfe had boiled it down to the plain question of how to break through the family interference and get the one with the ball. If Mrs. Whitten saw him coming, as she certainly did, and if she was determined to protect the flock even if one of them had killed her Floyd and taken a whack at her, her best bet was just to sit on it and not budge. But she wanted to do it her way, so she called Wolfe on the detail of lying to the cops.

Her point was that he couldn't possibly have learned anything about what happened Monday evening except from Pompa, and what would he expect from a man under arrest for murder? Jerome also had a point. Even if they had lied about the object of the meeting, which wasn't so, that was no proof, not even an indication, that one of them had killed Whitten. Would any group of people, having found Whitten dead upstairs, have admitted that they had met secretly to find ways and means of keeping him from getting what belonged to them? Though completely innocent, they would be fools so to complicate a simple situation—simple, because Pompa was obviously guilty, not only to them but to the police.

Wolfe let them make their points.

The questions and answers went on for two hours. It seemed to me like an awful waste of time and breath, since no matter what was fact and what was fancy, they were certainly all glued together on it and the glue had had two days to dry. The first interruption in the dining room Monday evening had been when Pompa had rung the doorbell. They hadn't known who it was, and had merely sat tight, supposing the bell ringer would depart. But in a few minutes had come the sound of the front door opening, and through the closed door of the dining room they could recognize voices in the reception hall and hear feet mounting the stairs. From there on they had talked in whispers and more about their immediate predicament than the object of the meeting. There were fierce arguments. Bahr had advocated ascending to the second floor in a body and going to the mat on it, but no one had supported him. Mortimer and Eve had wanted them to sneak out and go to the Bahr apartment, but were voted down on account of the risk of being seen from the upstairs windows. They spent the last hour sitting in the dark, hissing at one another, and Jerome had joined the Mortimer-and-Eve faction, making it a majority, when steps were heard descending the stairs, then, soon, other steps coming down fast, and Mrs. Whitten calling to Pompa. The voices were loud enough for them to hear words. After a door had closed and the voices were gone, a cautious reconnoiter by Phoebe had informed them that Pompa and Mrs. Whitten were in the living room. That had settled the argument about sneaking out, and the next event on the program, some half an hour later, had been the upsetting of a floor lamp by a careless movement in the dark by Bahr.

On the crucial question the glue held everywhere. Who had left the room after Pompa and Mrs. Whitten had entered the living room? Only Phoebe, for reconnaissance, and never for more than half a minute at a time. It didn't leave much elbow room for genius, not even Wolfe's. It was all well enough to remind them that it had been pitch dark, and to keep digging at where this one or that one had been, and what was Bahr doing when he upset the lamp, but if they were unanimous that they knew beyond doubt that no one had left the room except Phoebe for her brief excursions, what were you going to do, even if you knew in your bones that what they were really unanimous on was a resolution not to let one of them get tagged for murder? If what they had to be solid on had been some intricate series of events with a tricky time table, it might have been cracked open, but all they had to do was keep repeating that no one left the room during that half an hour except Phoebe, and that she wasn't out for more than thirty seconds at a time.

It was exactly the same for that evening, Wednesday, as it was for Monday. No fancy getup was required. They simply stated that they had all been in the house together for nearly an hour when the bell had rung and the butler had answered it, and Mrs. Whitten had staggered in with blood all over her. Again there was no place to start a wedge. Jerome, in his quiet subdued manner, offered to help by going to bring the butler, but Wolfe declined without thanks.

Wolfe glanced at the clock on the wall; it was a quarter to three. He tightened his lips and moved his eyes along the arc.

"Well. I am merely flattening my nose, to no purpose. We can't go on all night, ladies and gentlemen. You'd better go home and go to bed." He looked at Mrs. Whitten. "Except you, madam. You will of course sleep here. We have a spare room with a comfortable—"

There were protests in five voices, of various tones and tenors. Mortimer was of course the loudest, with Eve a close second. Wolfe shut his eyes while the storm blew, and then opened them.

"What do you think?" he demanded peevishly. "Am I a dunce? In a murder case it sometimes happens that a detective, stopped at a dead end, simply withdraws to wait upon a further event that may start a new path. That may be allowable, but not when the expected event is another murder. Not for me. A desire or intention to harm Mrs. Whitten may be in none of your minds, but I'm not going to risk it. She would be dead now if that blade had gone five inches in instead of across. I am willing, for the time being, to pursue this inquiry myself without recourse to the police or the District Attorney, but only with that condition: Mrs. Whitten stays under my roof until I am satisfied on certain points. She can leave at any moment if she regards the police as less obnoxious than me."

"If you ask me, they are," Eve snapped.

"This is blackmail and actionable," Bahr declared.

"Okay, she goes home and you call the goddam cops," was Mort's contribution.

"If she stays," Phoebe said firmly, "I stay."

Mrs. Whitten found use for a long deep sigh for about the thousandth time. Twice during the session I had been sure she was going to faint. But there was plenty of life in her eyes as she met Wolfe's gaze. "You said you would speak to me privately about Miss Alving."

"Yes, madam, I did."

"Then you could do that in the morning. I'm afraid I couldn't listen now—I'm pretty tired." Her hands, on her lap, tightened into fists and then relaxed. She turned to her younger daughter. "Phoebe, you'll have to go home and get things for us." She went back to Wolfe. "Your spare room—will it do for two?"

"Admirably. There are twin beds."

"Then my daughter Phoebe will be with me. I don't think you need to fear for my safety—I'm sure she won't kill me in my sleep. Tomorrow afternoon, if I'm still here, you will have to excuse me. My husband's funeral will be at four o'clock."

"Mother," Jerome said quietly, "let me take you home."

She didn't use breath to answer him, but asked Wolfe, "Will I have to walk upstairs?"

"No indeed," Wolfe said, as if that made everything fine and dandy. "You may use my elevator."

VIII

The fact is we have two spare rooms. Wolfe's room is at the rear of the house on the second floor, which he uses because its windows face south, and there is another bedroom on that floor in front, unoccupied. On the third floor my room is the one at the front, on the street, and there is another spare at the rear which we call the South Room. We put Mrs. Whitten and Phoebe there because it is large, and has better furniture and rugs, its own bathroom, and twin beds. I had told them where I could be found in case of fire.

I heard a noise. That put it up to me to decide whether I was awake or asleep, and I went to work on it. But I didn't feel like working and was going to let it slide when there was another noise.

"Mr. Goodwin."

Recognizing the name, I opened my eyes. An attractive young woman in a blue summer negligee, with hair the color of maple sirup, was standing at the foot of my bed. There was plenty of daylight from the windows to get details.

"I didn't knock," she said, "because I didn't want to disturb anyone."

"You've disturbed me," I asserted, swinging my legs around and sitting on the bed's edge. "What for?"

"I'm hungry."

I looked at my wrist. "My God, it'll be time for breakfast in three hours, and Fritz will bring it up to you. You don't look on the brink of starvation." She didn't. She looked all right.

"I can't sleep and I'm hungry."

"Then eat. The kitchen is on the same—" I stopped, having got enough awake to remember that (a) she was a guest and (b) I was a detective. I slipped my feet into my sandals, arose, told her, "Come on," and headed for the door. Halfway down the first flight I thought of a dressing gown, but it was too hot anyway.

Down in the kitchen I opened the door of the refrigerator and asked her, "Any special longing?"

"No, just food. Bread and meat and milk would be nice."

We got out an assortment: salami, half a Georgia ham, pâté, cheese, cucumber rings, Italian bread, and milk. She volunteered to slice some ham, and was very nifty at it. Now that she had broken my sleep I saw no reason to let her monopolize things, so I joined in. I took the stool and let her have the chair. I had happened to notice before that she had good teeth, and now I also noticed that they knew how to deal with bread and meat. She chewed as if she meant it, but with no offense.

We made conversation. "When I heard my name and opened my eyes and saw you," I told her, "I supposed it was one of two things. Either you had been drawn to my room as a moth to a candle, or you wanted to tell me something. When you said you were hungry it was a comedown. However—" I waved a hand, and on the way back it snared a slice of salami.

"I don't think there's much moth in me," she said. "And you're not so hot as a candle, with your hair like that and in those wrinkled pajamas. But I do want to tell you something. The hunger was just an opening."

"My pajamas always get wrinkled by the middle of the week no matter how careful I am. What's on your mind?"

She finished with a bite of cheese. Then she drank some milk. Then she arranged for her eyes to meet mine.   •

"We're more apt to do some good if you'll tell *me* something. What makes you think Pompa didn't kill Floyd Whitten?"

That got me wide awake and I hastily shifted things around inside my head. Up to then the emphasis had been on this interesting, informal, early-morning, intimate association with a really pretty specimen, but she had made it quite different. Having never seen H. R. Landy, I didn't know how much she looked like her father, but her manner and tone as she asked that question, and the look in her fine young eyes, had sure come straight from the man who had built up a ten-million-dollar business.

I grinned at her. "That's a swell way to repay me for getting up to feed you. If we have any evidence it's Mr. Wolfe's, not mine, so ask him. If we haven't any you wouldn't be interested."

"I might be. Try me."

"I wouldn't dream of boring you. More milk?"

"Then I'll bore you. I know Pompa pretty well. I have been with him a lot the past two years, working with him—I suppose you know that. He's an awful old tyrant in some ways, and he certainly is pig-headed, but I like him. I don't believe he would have killed Floyd Whitten for the only motive he had, and I know darned well he wouldn't have killed him by stabbing him in the back."

I frowned. "What kind of a dodge is this? You're out of my reach. Have you told that to the cops?"

"Of course not. I haven't told it to you, either, in case they ask me, and anyhow it's just my opinion. But that's what I think, and you see what it means. If Pompa didn't do it then one of us did, and I know we didn't. Or take it the way you're looking at it, that that's a lie, that we're all lying together—even so, there's no way on earth of proving we're lying, so it goes back on Pompa and he'll have to suffer for it. But I've told you what I think about him, and so I wonder if he has told the police all the details, and if they believe him. I would like to help him if I can—I mean it. Has he told about the front door being open?"

"I don't know. What front door, up at your house?"

She nodded. "As we told you, I left the room several times during that half-hour, to make sure Mother and Pompa were still in the living room. And each time, all the time, the front door wasn't closed. It was standing a little open. I supposed that when Mother came down to keep Pompa from going, he had already opened the front door to leave when she stopped him, and they neglected to close it when they went into the living room. That must have been it, because I had looked out there before, before Mother and Pompa came down, and so had Eve and Jerome, and the front door had been closed up to then."

I was letting the tingles inside of me enjoy themselves, and staying deadpan. "That's very interesting," I granted. "You've told about this, have you?"

"No, I haven't mentioned it. I don't know—I just didn't mention it. It didn't occur to me until this evening, from the questions Mr. Wolfe asked, how important it was. Of course the door being open meant that any time during that half-hour someone could have gone in and upstairs, and killed Floyd, and out again. So I wonder if Pompa has told about it. He must know it, since he must have opened the door himself and not closed it. I thought maybe he had told about it and they hadn't believed him. But they would have to believe him if I said I saw the door open too. Wouldn't they?"

"It would help," I conceded. "And of course it

would split it wide open. It would be a beautiful out, not only for Pompa, but for everybody. Two are much better than one, and three would be simply splendid. Do you suppose there's any chance that your mother remembers about the open door too?"

Her eyes left mine, and she covered up fairly well by reaching for the milk bottle and pouring herself a third of a glass. I didn't mark it against her, for she was too young to be expected to meet any and all contingencies.

"I sure was hungry and thirsty," she said, retrieving. "I don't know about Mother. I didn't ask her about it because she was completely all in. But when I tell her I saw it, and she puts her mind on it, I'm practically certain she'll remember about the door being open. She's very observant and she has a good memory. I don't think there's any question about her remembering it. That would clear up everything, wouldn't it?"

"It would at least scatter the clouds all over the sky," I conceded. "What would be even sweeter would be if the first couple of times you ventured forth you noticed the door was open, and the last time you saw it had been closed. That would be really jolly. You probably have a good memory too, so why don't you try it on that?"

But she wasn't having any fancy touches from comparative strangers. Nope, she remembered it quite clearly, the door had been open all the time. Furthermore, she remembered going to close it herself, when her mother and brother and Dan Bahr had gone upstairs to get Floyd Whitten. I didn't think it would be polite to urge her, and while we were cleaning up and putting things back in the refrigerator I told her that it was darned white of her to come out with it like that, and this was a real break for Pompa, and I would give Wolfe the good news just as soon as he was awake. We went back up the two flights together, and in the upper hall I took her offered hand and got a fine firm clasp and a friendly smile. Then I went back to bed and was sound asleep before I knew it.

My eyes opened again without any order from me. Naturally that was irritating, and I wondered why I couldn't sleep. Seeing it was broad daylight, I glanced at my wrist. It was a quarter past nine. I jumped out and leaped for the bathroom, set a record dressing, ran down to the kitchen, and asked Fritz if Wolfe was awake. Yes, he had breakfasted at eight-fifteen as usual and was up in the plant rooms. There had just been word from the South Room, on the house phone, from the guests, and Fritz was getting their trays ready. On account of my snack at dawn I wasn't starving, so I had my orange juice and some toast and coffee, and then went, three steps at a time, up to the roof.

Wolfe was in the intermediate room inspecting some two-year Miltonia roezelis. The brief glance he gave me was as sour as expected, since he hates being interrupted up there.

I apologized without groveling. "I'm sorry I overslept, but it was Phoebe's fault. She has a nerve. She came to my room, and damned if she didn't complain about my wrinkled pajamas."

He dehydrated me with a look. "If true, boorish. If false, inane."

"Just adjectives. She came because she was hungry, and I took her down and fed her. But what she really wanted was to peddle a lie. Would you care to buy a good lie? It's a beaut."

"Describe it."

"She offers to trade an out for Pompa for an out for the dining-room gang. During that crucial half-hour, each time she sallied to the reception hall she noticed that the front door was part way open. Mama will corroborate. But Pompa will have to say that when he started to beat it he got as far as the front door and had opened it when Mom caught up with him, and neither of them closed it before they went into the living room. Which is that, boorish or inane?"

Wolfe finished inspecting a plant, returned it to the bench, and turned to inspect me. He seemed to have a notion there was something wrong with my necktie, as there may well have been since I had set a record.

"What inspired you to use Miss Alving's name to get in to Mrs. Whitten?" he demanded.

"Hell, I had to use something. Knowing how women are apt to feel about their husbands' former sweethearts, I thought that was as good as anything and probably better."

"Was that all?"

"Yep. Why, did I spill salt?"

"No. On the contrary. Do you know where Miss Alving can be found?"

I nodded. "She's the toy buyer at Meadow's. But you certainly have changed the subject. What about that Grade A lie, do we want it at the price? Phoebe will be after me as soon as she gets through breakfast."

"We'll see. That can wait. How do you know it's a lie? Come in the potting room where we can sit down. I have some instructions."

IX

Never to find yourself in a situation where you have to enter a big department store is one of the minor reasons for not getting married. I guess it would also be a reason for not being a detective. Anyway, Meadow's is unquestionably a big department store, and that Thursday morning I had to enter it in the practice of my profession. The toy department is on the fourth floor, I suppose to give the kids more fun on the escalators. By the time I got there the sweat on my back was starting to freeze in the conditioned air, and I had to resist an impulse to go up another flight and buy a topcoat.

The salesperson I approached said she thought Miss Alving was busy and would I wait. I found an empty chair over by the scooters. I thought contact with the chair's back might melt the ice on mine, but it was plastic, so I sat straight. After a while a woman came hurrying to me, and I arose.

"Miss Julie Alving?"

"Yes, I'm Miss Alving."

When Marko had told us about Floyd Whitten's former love whom he had ditched when he married the boss, I had made a casual mental comment that there was something droll about a man living in sin with a toy buyer, but one look at Julie Alving showed me that such casual comments can be silly. She was forty and looked it, and she was not an eyestopper in any obvious way, but everything about her, the way she walked, the way she stood, her eyes and mouth and whole face, seemed to be saying, without trying or intending to, that if you had happened to be hers, and she yours, life would be full of pleasant and interesting surprises. It wasn't anything personal, it was just her. I was so impressed, in spite of her age, that I was smiling at her before I knew it.

I spoke. "My name's Archie Goodwin, Miss Alving, and I work for Nero Wolfe. You may have heard of him? The detective?"

"Yes, I've heard of him." Her voice was a little thin.

"He would like to see you. He would appreciate it very much if you can get away for an hour and come to his office with me. He has something to say to you on behalf of Mrs. Floyd Whitten."

I thought for a second she was going to topple. The way her head jerked up and then came down again as all her muscles sagged, it was as if I had landed an uppercut. My hand even started to reach, to be there if the muscles really quit, but she stayed upright.

"Mrs.—Mrs. Whitten?" she stammered.

I nodded. "You used to know her husband. Here, sit down."

She ignored that. "What does she want?"

"I don't know, but Mr. Wolfe does. She came to see him last night and they talked. He said to tell you it's important and urgent, and he has to see you this morning."

"But I—I'm here at work."

"Yeah, I know. I work too and know how it is. I told him you might not be able to make it until after the store closes, but he said that wouldn't do."

"What did Mrs. Whitten talk to him about?"

I shook my head. "You'll have to ask him."

She got her teeth on her lower lip, kept them there a while, said, "Wait here, please," and left me. She passed behind a counter and disappeared through a partition opening. I sat down. When my watch showed me that I had waited twenty-two minutes I began to wonder if I was being imposed on, but no, she returned.

She came to me and said, "I'll leave right away. What's the address?"

I told her we might as well go together, and when she objected that she must go out by the employees' entrance I hurdled that by arranging for us to meet outside. My instructions were to bring her, and I'm great for instructions. My guesses on the role Wolfe was casting her for were nothing but guesses, and they contradicted one another, but if by any chance he had her down for top billing I didn't want to be responsible for her not showing up. So I was really pleased to see her when she reached the meeting place on the sidewalk not more than a minute after I did.

On the way down in the taxi she sat with a tight two-handed grip on her bag, and had no comments or questions. That suited me, since I hadn't the faintest idea what she was heading into and therefore would have been able to make no contribution except grunts.

Since I had been instructed not to tell her that Mrs. Whitten and Phoebe were our house guests, I wouldn't have been surprised to see them both there in the office when I entered with Julie Alving, but Wolfe was alone, in his chair behind his desk, with a newspaper. He put the paper down, got to his feet, and bowed, which was quite a tribute, either to Julie or the part she was supposed to take. I've seen him react to a woman's entrance in that office with nothing but a ferocious scowl. So I participated by giving Miss Alving the red leather chair.

She sat, still clutching her bag, and gazed at him. Wolfe told me to get my notebook and I did so. A man getting a notebook and pen ready sometimes makes quite an effect.

Wolfe returned her gaze. "I suppose Mr. Goodwin told you that I wanted to speak with you about Mrs. Whitten."

She nodded. "Yes, that's what he said—no, he said on behalf of Mrs. Whitten."

Wolfe waved it away with a finger. "He may have used that phrase. He likes it. In any case, I'll come straight to the point. I think I can arrange it so that Mrs. Whitten will not prosecute, if you'll help me."

"Prosecute?" She was only so-so at faking surprise. "Prosecute who?"

"You, Miss Alving. Have you no notion of what charge Mrs. Whitten can lay against you?"

"Certainly not. There isn't any."

"When did you last see her?"

"I never have seen her—that is, I've never met her."

"When did you last see her?"

"I don't know—a long while—months ago. I only saw her two or three times—never to speak to."

"That was months ago?"

"Yes."

"Do you owe her anything?"

"No."

"Does she owe you anything?"

"No."

"Have you ever had anything to do with her—anything at all?"

"No."

"Have you any reason to expect or fear anything from her, good or bad?"

"No."

"Then will you please tell me why, when Mr. Goodwin told you I wanted to speak with you on behalf of Mrs. Whitten, you left your work immediately and came here with him?"

Julie looked at him, and then at me as if it was up to me to answer that one. Seeing that I was no nearer ready with something adequate than she was, she went back to Wolfe.

"Why wouldn't I?" she demanded. "After what has happened, wouldn't I want to know what she wanted?"

Wolfe nodded approvingly. "That was much the best you could do, and you did it. But it's not good enough. If you maintain this attitude, Miss Alving, I'm afraid I'm out of it, and you'll have others to deal with. I would advise you to reconsider. I think you're wrong to assume that they will believe you, and not Mrs. Whitten, when she tells them that you attacked her with a knife and your target was her heart."

"I didn't!" Julie cried. That was only so-so too.

"Nonsense. Of course you did. I can understand your reluctance, since nothing has been published about it, and for all you know Mrs. Whitten may be at the point of death. But she isn't. Your blade didn't get beyond the rib, and twelve stitches were all that was necessary to make her capable of riding here to my office. Except for a little loss of blood she's as good as ever. She hasn't even reported it to the police, not wishing to give the public another mouthful to chew on—a mortal assault on her by the former friend of her murdered husband. So the limit of a charge against you would be assault with intent to kill."

Wolfe waved that aside as if it were a mere peccadillo. "And if you'll be frank with me and answer some questions, I undertake to arrange that Mrs. Whitten will not prosecute. If you had achieved your purpose, if she were dead, that would be different and I wouldn't be so foolish as to expect frankness from you. I wouldn't ask you to confess a murder, Miss Alving."

She was doing her best and I admired her for it. But the trouble was that she had to decide on her line right there facing us, and having to make up your mind with Nero Wolfe's eyes, open an eighth of an inch, on you, is no situation for an amateur.

However, she wasn't made of jelly. "When did this —when and where was Mrs. Whitten attacked?"

"I'll refresh your memory," Wolfe said patiently, "if you want it that way. A quarter to ten last evening, in front of her house, as she got out of her car."

"It wasn't in the papers. I should think a thing like that would be in the papers."

"Only if the papers heard of it, and they didn't. Naturally you searched for it. I've told you why Mrs. Whitten didn't report it."

Julie was still making up her mind. "It seems to me you're expecting a good deal—I mean, even if I did it, and I didn't. If I had, the way it looks to me, I wouldn't know whether you were trying to get me to confess to a murder or not. I wouldn't know whether she were dead, or had just lost some blood as you said. Would I?"

She had him there. He sat and gazed at her a long moment, grunted, and turned to me.

"Archie. Bring that witness down here. Only the one. If the other one is importunate, remind her that I said our talk about Miss Alving must be tête-à-tête."

X

Phoebe wasn't importunate. When I entered the South Room on the third floor she was talking on the phone, that extension having been plugged in for an outside line, and her mother was sitting in a chair by the window with a newspaper on her lap. She arose at once, with no need for assistance, when I said Wolfe was ready for their private talk, and Phoebe, having finished on the phone, had no comment on that, but she wanted to know what I had for her. I told her she would be hearing from me shortly, or more probably from Wolfe, and escorted Mrs. Whitten to the elevator, which I never used except when I was convoying casualties, and out at the lower hall and into the office.

I kept right at her elbow because I didn't want to miss the expression on Julie Alving's face when she saw her. It was first just plain surprise and then a mixture in which the only ingredient I could positively label was just plain hate. As for Mrs. Whitten, I had only her profile from a corner of my eye, but she stopped dead and went as stiff as a steel beam.

Wolfe spoke. "This is my witness, Miss Alving. I believe you ladies haven't met. Mrs. Whitten, Miss Alving."

Mrs. Whitten moved, and for a second I thought she was turning to march out, but she was merely reaching for a hold on my sleeve. I took her arm and herded her left oblique. Being wounded, she rated the red leather chair, but it seemed inadvisable to ask Julie to move, so I took the witness to a yellow one with arms, not as roomy but just as comfortable. When she was in it I resumed my post at my desk with notebook and pen.

"I'm sorry," Wolfe said, "if it makes a queasy atmosphere, you two here together, but Miss Alving left me no alternative." He focused on Mrs. Whitten. "I was having a little trouble with Miss Alving. I wanted her to talk about certain aspects of the assault she made on you last evening, but she wouldn't have it—and I don't blame her—because she didn't know how badly you were hurt. There was only one way to handle it—let her see for herself."

I had to hand it to him. He not only wasn't taking too big a risk, he was taking none at all, since they weren't on speaking terms.

"How did you find out it was her?" Mrs. Whitten demanded. Her voice was harsh and high-pitched.

"Oh, that was simple. I'll tell you presently. But first we should understand one another. I appreciate your reason for not wanting it bruited, and sympathize with it, but here in private there should be candor. You positively recognized her?"

"Certainly I did."

"Beyond possibility of doubt?"

"Certainly. I saw her face when I got turned and that was when she tore loose and ran. And she spoke to me."

"What did she say?"

"I'm not sure of the words, but it was something like 'I'll kill you too.' That's what I thought it was, but later I thought it must be wrong because I thought Pompa had killed my husband and I didn't realize she could have done it. But now that my daughter remembers about the open door, and I remember it too, I see that must have been it—what she said."

"That's a lie!" Julie blurted, not at Mrs. Whitten, since she wasn't speaking to her, but at Wolfe. She was fully as pale as Mrs. Whitten had been the evening before, but not like a corpse, anything but. She was blurting on. "I didn't say that! I said 'You killed him and I'll kill you!' And I wish I had—oh, I wish I had!"

"You came close to it," Wolfe growled. He let his eyes come halfway open, now that he had them. "I should explain to both of you that I've merely been trying to get started. Please forget each other, as far as possible, and listen to me. If we're going to work this out together you need to know how I got where I am now."

The doorbell rang. Under the circumstances it was up to Fritz, but on the other hand we didn't want any trivial interruptions just then, so I scooted for the hall, closing the office doors as I went. One glance through the glass panel showed that my point was well taken. Inspector Cramer was there. He was alone, so I didn't bother with the chain bolt but put my foot where it would keep the door to a six-inch crack. I spoke through the crack to his big broad shoulders and his round, red, but by no means flabby face.

"Good morning. What have I done now?"

"We sent a man," he snapped, "to see Mrs. Whitten about something, and he was told she's here. What's Wolfe up to? I want to see her."

"I never know what he's up to, but I'll go ask him. He'll want to know how it stands. Is there a warrant for her?"

"Hell no. A warrant for what?"

"I merely asked. Kindly withdraw your toe."

I banged the door shut, went to the office, and told Wolfe, "The man about the chair. The one with a gash in it. He learned more or less accidentally that it's here, and that made him curious, and he wants to talk.

He has no signed paper and no idea of getting one.
Shall I tell him you're busy?"

I was sure he would say yes, but he didn't. Instead, he decoded it. "Is it Mr. Cramer?"

"Yes, sir." He knew darned well it was, since I had
started years ago calling Cramer that.

"He wants to speak with Mrs. Whitten?"

"One of his did, probably about some trifle,
and found out she was here. What he really wants is
to see if you're getting up a charade."

"He's barely in time. If he engages to let me proceed without interruption until I've finished, admit
him."

"I don't like it. He's got Pompa."

"He won't have him long. We're waiting for you. I
want a record of this."

I didn't like it at all, but when Wolfe has broken
into a gallop what I like has about the weight of an
undersized feather from a chicken's neck.

I returned to the front and opened to a crack again
and told the inspector, "Mrs. Whitten is in the office
with him, chatting. So is Miss Julie Alving, toy buyer
at Meadow's, who was formerly on good terms with
the late Whitten. You may have heard of her."

"Yeah, I have. What the hell is he trying to pull?"

"You name it. I'm just the stenographer. You have
a choice. Being an inspector, you can go somewhere
for lunch and then take in a ball game, or you can give
me your sacred word of honor that you'll absolutely
keep your mouth shut until and unless Wolfe hands
you the torch. If you choose the latter you're welcome, and you can have a chair to sit on. After all, you
have no ticket even for standing room, since neither
of those females is under a charge."

"I'm a police officer. I'm not going to tie myself—"

"Don't haggle. You know damn well where you stand. I'm needed in there to take notes. Well?"

"I'm coming in."

"Under the terms as I stated?"

"Yes."

"Strictly clam?"

"Yes."

"Okay. Otherwise you'd better bring a bulldozer if you ever want in again." I swung the door open.

Wolfe greeted him curtly and left it to me to introduce him to the ladies. It wasn't surprising that he hadn't met Mrs. Whitten, since his men had settled on Pompa as a cinch after a few hours' investigation and therefore there had been no occasion for their superior officer to annoy the widow. He acknowledged the introductions with stingy nods, gave Wolfe a swift keen glance that would have liked to go on through his hide to the interior, and indicated that he intended to keep his vow by taking a chair well out of it, to the rear and right of Mrs. Whitten.

Wolfe spoke to him. "Let's put it this way, Mr. Cramer. You're here merely as a caller waiting to see me."

"That will do," Cramer growled.

"Good. Then I'll proceed. I was just starting to explain to these ladies the manner and extent of my progress in an investigation I'm on."

"Go ahead."

From there on Wolfe ignored Cramer completely. He looked at Julie and Mrs. Whitten. "What persuaded me," he said conversationally, "of Mr. Pompa's innocence, and who engaged me to prove it, are details of no importance. Neither is it important why, when Mr. Goodwin wanted to contrive an entree to

Mrs. Whitten, he hit on the stratagem of saying he wished to speak with her on behalf of Miss Alving."

Julie made a sound.

"Oh, it was a lie," he told her. "We use a great many of them in this business, sometimes calculated with great care, sometimes quite at random. This one was extremely effective. It got Mr. Goodwin admitted to Mrs. Whitten at once, though she was in bed with a gash in her side, having just narrowly escaped from an attempt on her life."

Cramer let out a growl, no doubt involuntary, and stood up. Wolfe ignored him and went on to his female audience.

"That, of course, is news to Mr. Cramer, and there will be more for him, but since he's merely waiting to see me I'll finish with you ladies. The success—"

"You not only lie," Mrs. Whitten said harshly, "you break your promise. You promised that if we answered your questions you wouldn't report the attack on me to the police."

"No," Wolfe said curtly. "I do not break promises. It was implied, not explicit, and it was without term, and assuredly not for eternity. Certainly I could not be expected to keep that information to myself if and when it became necessary evidence for the disclosure of a murderer. It has now become necessary."

"It has?" She wasn't so harsh.

"Yes."

"Then—go on."

He did. "The success of Mr. Goodwin's device for getting to Mrs. Whitten was highly suggestive. True, her husband had been intimate with Miss Alving at one time, but he had discarded her before his marriage. Then why should the name of Miss Alving get quick entry to Mrs. Whitten at such a moment? There had to be a good reason, but I could only guess. Among my guesses was the possibility that the assault on Mrs. Whitten had been made by Miss Alving, but that's all it was at the time, one of a string of guesses. However, when Mr. Goodwin reported that detail to me we already had a good deal more. He had, in a keen and rapid stroke, discovered why Mrs. Whitten had been put to bed by a doctor, and, on account of her determination not to let it be known, had provided us with a powerful instrument to use on her. It was indeed powerful. It got her out of bed after midnight and brought her down here to see me, accompanied by her family."

"When, last night?" Cramer demanded.

Wolfe glared at him. "Sir, you are committed. Later you'll get all you want. Now I'm working."

"Who told you he discarded me?" Julie asked. I thought her voice sounded much like Mrs. Whitten's, and then I realized that it wasn't the voices that were similar, it was the emotions. It was hate.

"The source was Mr. Pompa," Wolfe told her. "If the word was unfortunate and offends you, I am sorry. It may not fit the occasion at all. To go on. Last evening, looking at those people and hearing them, I concluded that none of them was capable of trying to kill their mother. I couldn't exclude the possibility, but I could tentatively reject it, and I did. But that brought Miss Alving in again. Mrs. Whitten claimed that not only could she not identify her assailant, she didn't even know whether it was a man or a woman. That was absurd. It was of course intrinsically improbable, but it was made absurd by the question, if she had no idea who the attacker was why was she going to such lengths to keep the incident from disclosure? Even leaving her bed to come to see me in the

dead of night? Therefore she knew who had attacked
her, and desperately wanted no one else to know. I
excluded her children, as I have said, whom she might
have shielded through love or pride, and I knew of no
one else in that category. But not only love rides with
pride; hate also does. There was Miss Alving again."

Wolfe shook his head. "Miss Alving was still only a
guess, though now a much more likely one. It was
worth having a try at her. The device Mr. Goodwin
had used on Mrs. Whitten got an encore. He went to
see Miss Alving and told her that I wished to speak
with her on behalf of Mrs. Whitten. It worked beauti-
fully. For a department buyer in a great department
store to leave her post in the middle of the morning on
her private affairs is by no means routine or casual,
but Miss Alving did that. She came here at once with
Mr. Goodwin. My guess was now good enough to put
to the test, and Miss Alving's reaction removed all
doubt, though she did her best. Mr. Goodwin brought
Mrs. Whitten down, and that made the situation impossible for both of you. You have both admitted that
the attack on Mrs. Whitten was made by Miss Alving.
That is true, Miss Alving?"

"Yes." Julie tried to swallow. "I wish I had killed
her."

"A very silly wish. It is true, Mrs. Whitten?"

"Yes." Mrs. Whitten's expression was not a wishing one. "I didn't want it to be known because I knew
—I knew my husband wouldn't. I hadn't thought of
the open door, and so I didn't realize that she had
killed him. She had waited for six long months, waited
and hoped, hoping to get him back." Mrs. Whitten's
eyes left Wolfe, and they were hot with hate and accusation as they fixed on Julie. "But you couldn't! He

was mine, and you couldn't have him! So you killed him!"

"That's a lie," Julie said, deadly quiet and low. "It's a lie and you know it. I did have him. He was mine all the time, and you knew it. You found it out."

Wolfe pounced. "What's that?" he snapped. "She found it out?"

"Yes."

"Look at me, Miss Alving. Let her go. Look at me. You are in no danger; there was no open door. When did she find it out?"

Julie's head had slowly turned to face him. "A month ago."

"How do you know?"

"He wrote me that he didn't dare to come—where we met—because she had learned about it. He was afraid, terribly afraid of her. I knew he was a coward. Don't ever fall in love with a coward."

"I'll guard against it. Have you got the letter?"

She nodded. The pallor was gone and her face was flushed, but her voice was quiet and dull. "I have all of them. He wrote eleven letters in that month, but I never saw him again. He kept saying he would come soon, and he would as soon as he could, but he was a coward."

"Did he tell you how she learned about it?"

"Yes, it was in the first letter."

"And when he died, and you knew she had killed him, you thought you would avenge him yourself, was that it?"

"Yes. What else could I do?"

"You might—but no matter. You loved him?"

"I do love him."

"Did he love you?"

"Yes—oh, yes!"

"Better than he loved his wife?"

"He hated her. He despised her. He laughed at her."

Mrs. Whitten made a choking noise and was out of her chair. But I, rather expecting a little something, was on my feet too, and in front of her. She started to stretch a hand to me and then sat down again. Thinking it remotely possible that she had a cutlery sample in her bag, I stood by.

Wolfe spoke to her. "I should tell you, madam, that I've had you in mind from the first. When you discovered your family secretly gathered in the dining room you were not yourself. Instead of upbraiding and bullying them, which would have been in character, you appealed to them. What better explanation could there be of that reversal in form than that you knew your husband was upstairs dead, you having killed him with one swift stab in the back as you passed behind him, leaving him to go down after Mr. Pompa? Your shrewd and careful plan to have it laid to Pompa was badly disarranged by the awful discovery that your sons and daughters were there too; no wonder you were upset. Your plan was not only shrewd and careful, but long and deep, for when, a month ago, you learned of your husband's infidelity, what did you do? Drive him out with a blast of fury and contempt? No. Understand him and forgive him and try to win him all for you? No. You displayed the blooming and ripening of your affection and trust for him by announcing that he was to be put in control of the family business. That made it certain, you thought, that when you chose your moment and he died, you would be above suspicion. And indeed you were, but you had bad luck. It was ruthless, but wise, to arrange for the police to have a victim at hand, but you had the misfortune to

select for that role a man who was once a good cook—
indeed, a great one."

Wolfe jerked his head up. "Mr. Cramer, you are no
longer committed. I don't know how you handle a case
like this. You have a man in jail charged with murder,
but the murderer is here. How do you proceed?"

"I need things," Cramer rasped. He was flabbergasted and trying not to show it. "I need those letters.
What's that about an open door? I need—"

"You'll get all of it. I mean what happens immediately? What about Mrs. Whitten?"

"That's no problem. There are two men in my car
out front. If her wound didn't keep her from riding
down here last night it won't keep her from riding
downtown now."

"Good." Wolfe turned to Julie. "I was under an
obligation to you. I told you that I thought I could
arrange it so that Mrs. Whitten would not prosecute,
if you would help me. You have unquestionably helped
me. You have done your part. Do you agree that I
have done mine?"

I don't think she heard a word of it. She was looking at him but not seeing him. "There was a notice in
yesterday's paper," she said, "that his funeral would
be today at four o'clock, and it said omit flowers. Omit
flowers!" She seemed to be trying to smile, and suddenly her head dropped into her hands and she shook
with sobs.

XI

I stood facing the door of the South Room, in the hall
on the third floor, with my hand raised. Wolfe, posi-

tively refusing to do it himself, had left it to me. I
knocked. A voice told me to come in, and I entered.

Phoebe tossed a magazine onto the table and left
the chair. "You certainly took long enough. Where's
Mother?"

"That's what I came to tell you."

Her face changed and she took a step and demanded, "Where is she?"

"Don't push. First I apologize. When you pulled
that gag about the front door being open I thought
you knew that one of you in the dining room had killed
Whitten, and possibly even you had been involved in
it, and you thought maybe Mr. Wolfe was getting
warm and you wanted to fix an out. Now I know how
it was. You couldn't believe Pompa had done it, and
you knew none of you had, so it was your mother. So
it was her you wanted the out for. Therefore it seems
to me I should apologize, and I do."

"I don't want your apology. Where is my mother?"

"She is either at Police Headquarters or the District Attorney's office, depending on where they took
her. I don't know. She is, or soon will be, charged with
murder. Mr. Wolfe did most of it of course, but I had a
hand in it. For that I don't apologize. You know damn
well she's a malicious and dangerous woman—look at
her framing Pompa—and while I appreciate the fact
that she's your mother, she is not mine. So much for
her. You are another matter. What do you want me to
do? Anything?"

"No."

She hadn't batted an eyelash, nor turned pale, nor
let a lip quiver, but the expression of her eyes was
plenty.

"What I mean," I told her, "I got you down here,
and you're here alone now, and I would like to do

anything at all that will help. Phone somebody, drive you somewhere, get a taxi, send your things to you later—"

"No."

"Okay. Fritz will let you out downstairs. I'll be in the office typing, in case."

That was the last chat I had with her for a long time, until day before yesterday, a month after her mother was sentenced by Judge Wilkinson. Day before yesterday, Tuesday afternoon, she phoned to say she had changed her mind about accepting my apology, and would I care to drive her up to Connecticut and eat dinner with her at AMBROSIA 26? Even if I hadn't had another date I would have passed. An AMBROSIA may be perfectly okay as a source of income, but with the crowd and the noise it is no place to make any progress in human relations.

Door to Death

Nero Wolfe took a long stretching step to clear a puddle of water at the edge of the graveled driveway, barely reached the grass of the lawn with his left foot, slipped, teetered, pawed wildly at the air, and got his sixth of a ton of flesh and bone balanced again without having actually sprawled.

"Just like Ray Bolger," I said admiringly.

He scowled at me savagely, which made me feel at home though we were far from home. More than an hour of that raw and wet December morning had been spent by me driving up to northern Westchester, with him in the rear seat on account of his silly theory that when the inevitable crash comes he'll lose less blood and have fewer bones broken, and there we were at our destination in the environs of the village of Katonah, trespassers on the estate of one Joseph G. Pitcairn. I say trespassers because, instead of wheeling up to the front of the big old stone mansion and crossing the terrace to the door like gentlemen, I had, under orders, branched off onto the service drive, circled to the rear of the house, and stopped the car at the gravel's edge in the neighborhood of the garage. The reason for that maneuver was that, far from being there to see Mr. Pitcairn, we were there to steal something from him.

"That was a fine recovery," I told Wolfe approvingly. "You're not used to this rough cross-country going."

Before he could thank me for the compliment a man in greasy coveralls emerged from the garage and came for us. It didn't seem likely, in view of the greasy coveralls, that he was what we had come to steal, but Wolfe's need was desperate and he was taking no chances, so he wiped the scowl off and spoke to the man in hearty friendliness.

"Good morning, sir."

The man nodded. "Looking for someone?"

"Yes, Mr. Andrew Krasicki. Are you him?"

"I am not. My name's Imbrie, Neil Imbrie, butler and chauffeur and handyman. You look like some kind of a salesman. Insurance?"

Butlers were entirely different, I decided, when you came at them by the back way. When Wolfe, showing no resentment at the accusation, whatever he felt, told him it wasn't insurance but something personal and agreeable, he took us to the far end of the garage, which had doors for five cars, and pointed out a path which wound off into shrubbery.

"That goes to his cottage, way the other side of the tennis court. In the summer you can't see it from here on account of the leaves, but now you can a little. He's down there taking a nap because he was up last night fumigating. Often I'm up late driving, but it don't mean I get a nap. The next time around I'm going to be a gardener."

Wolfe thanked him and made for the path, with me

for rearguard. It had just about made up its mind to stop raining, but everything was soaking wet, and after we got into the shrubbery we had to duck whenever a bare twig stretched out low to avoid making our own private rain. For me, young and limber and in good trim, that was nothing, but for Wolfe, with his three hundred pounds, which is an understatement, especially with his heavy tweed overcoat and hat and cane, it was asking a lot. The shrubbery quit at the other side of the tennis court, and we entered a grove of evergreens, then an open space, and there was the cottage.

Wolfe knocked on the door, and it opened, and facing us was a blond athlete not much older than me, with big bright blue eyes and his whole face ready to laugh. I never completely understand why a girl looks in any other direction when I am present, but I wouldn't have given it a moment's thought if this specimen had been in sight. Wolfe told him good morning and asked if he was Mr. Andrew Krasicki.

"That's my name." He made a little bow. "And may I—by God, it's Nero Wolfe! Aren't you Nero Wolfe?"

"Yes," Wolfe confessed modestly. "May I come in for a little talk, Mr. Krasicki? I wrote you a letter but got no reply, and yesterday on the telephone you—"

The blond prince interrupted. "It's all right," he declared. "All settled!"

"Indeed. What is?"

"I've decided to accept. I've just written you a letter."

"When can you come?"

"Any time you say. Tomorrow. I've got a good assistant and he can take over here."

Wolfe did not whoop with glee. Instead, he compressed his lips and breathed deep through his nose. In a moment he spoke. "Confound it, may I come in? I want to sit down."

II

Wolfe's reaction was perfectly natural. True, he had just got wonderful news, but also he had just learned that if he had stayed home he would have got it just the same in tomorrow morning's mail, and that was hard to take standing up. He hates going outdoors and rarely does, and he would rather trust himself in a room alone with three or four mortal enemies than in a piece of machinery on wheels.

But he had been driven to the wall. Four people live in the old brownstone house on West 35th Street. First, him. Second, me, assistant everything from detective to doorbell answerer. Third, Fritz Brenner, cook and house manager. And fourth, Theodore Horstmann, tender and defender of the ten thousand orchids in the plant rooms on the roof. But that was the trouble: there was no longer a fourth. A telegram had come from Illinois that Theodore's mother was critically ill and he must come at once, and he had taken the first train. Wolfe, instead of spending a pleasant four hours a day in the plant rooms pretending he was hard at it, had had to dig in and work like a dog. Fritz and I could help some, but we weren't experts. Appeals were broadcast in every direction, especially after word came from Theodore that he couldn't tell whether he would be back in six days or six months, and there were candidates for the job, but no one that Wolfe would trust with his rare and precious hybrids. He had already heard of this Andrew

Krasicki, who had successfully crossed an Odontoglossum cirrhosum with an O. nobile veitchianum, and when he learned from Lewis Hewitt that Krasicki had worked for him for three years and was as good as they come, that settled it. He had to have Krasicki. He had written him; no answer. He had phoned, and had been brushed off. He had phoned again, and got no further. So, that wet December morning, tired and peevish and desperate, he had sent me to the garage for the car, and when I rolled up in front of the house there he was on the sidewalk, in his hat and overcoat and cane, grim and resolute, ready to do or die. Stanley making for Livingstone in the African jungle was nothing compared to Wolfe making for Krasicki in Westchester.

And here was Krasicki saying he had already written he would come! It was an awful anticlimax.

"I want to sit down," Wolfe repeated firmly.

But he didn't get to, not yet. Krasicki said sure, go on in and make himself at home, but he had just been starting for the greenhouse when we arrived and he would have to go. I put in to remark that maybe we'd better get back to town, to our own greenhouse, and start the day's work. That reminded Wolfe that I was there, and he gave Krasicki and me each other's names, and we shook hands. Then Krasicki said he had a Phalaenopsis Aphrodite in flower we might like to see.

Wolfe grunted. "Species? I have eight."

"Oh, no." It was easy to tell from Krasicki's tone of horticultural snobbery, by no means new to me, that he really belonged. "Not species and not dayana. Sanderiana. Nineteen sprays."

"Good heavens," Wolfe said enviously. "I must see it."

So we neither went in and sat down nor went back to our car, which was just as well, since in either case we would have been minus a replacement for Theodore. Krasicki led the way along the path by which we had come, but as we approached the house and outbuildings he took a fork to the left which skirted shrubs and perennial borders, now mostly bare but all neat. As we passed a young man in a rainbow shirt who was scattering peat moss on a border, he said, "You owe me a dime, Andy. No snow," and Krasicki grinned and told him, "See my lawyer, Gus."

The greenhouse, on the south side of the house, had been hidden from our view as we had driven in. Approaching it even on this surly December day, it stole the show from the mansion. With stone base walls to match the house, and curving glass, it was certainly high, wide, and handsome. At its outer extremity it ended in a one-story stone building with a slate roof, and the path Krasicki took led to that, and around to its door. The whole end wall was covered with ivy, and the door was fancy, stained oak slabs decorated with black iron, and on it was hanging a big framed placard, with red lettering so big you could read it from twenty paces:

DANGER

DO NOT ENTER

DOOR TO DEATH

I muttered something about a cheerful welcome. Wolfe cocked an eye at the sign and asked, "Cyanogas G?"

Krasicki, lifting the sign from its hook and putting a key in the hole, shook his head. "Ciphogene. That's all right; the vents have been open for several hours.

This sign's a little poetic, but it was here when I came. I understand Mrs. Pitcairn painted it herself."

Inside with them, I took a good sniff of the air. Ciphogene is the fumigant Wolfe uses in his plant rooms, and I knew how deadly it was, but there was only a faint trace to my nose, so I went on breathing. The inside of the stone building was the storage and workroom, and right away Wolfe started looking things over.

Andy Krasicki said politely but briskly, "If you'll excuse me, I'm always behind a morning after fumigating . . ."

Wolfe, on his good behavior, followed him through the door into the greenhouse, and I went along.

"This is the cool room," Krasicki told us. "Next is the warm room, and then, the one adjoining the house, the medium. I have to get some vents closed and put the automatic on."

It was quite a show, no question about that, but I was so used to Wolfe's arrangement, practically all orchids, that it seemed pretty messy. When we proceeded to the warm room there was a sight I really enjoyed: Wolfe's face as he gazed at the P. Aphrodite sanderiana with its nineteen sprays. The admiration and the envy together made his eyes gleam as I had seldom seen them. As for the flower, it was new to me, and it was something special—rose, brown, purple, and yellow. The rose suffused the petals, and the brown, purple, and yellow were on the labellum.

"Is it yours?" Wolfe demanded.

Andy shrugged. "Mr. Pitcairn owns it."

"I don't care a hang who owns it. Who grew it?"

"I did. From a seed."

Wolfe grunted. "Mr. Krasicki, I'd like to shake your hand."

Andy permitted him to do so and then moved along to proceed through the door into the medium room, presumably to close more vents. After Wolfe had spent a few more minutes coveting the Phalaenopsis, we followed. This was another mess, everything from violet geraniums to a thing in a tub with eight million little white flowers, labeled Serissa foetida. I smelled it, got nothing, crushed one of the flowers with my fingers and smelled that, and then had no trouble understanding the foetida. My fingers had it good, so I went out to the sink in the workroom and washed with soap.

I got back to the medium room in time to hear Andy telling Wolfe that he had a curiosity he might like to see. "Of course," Andy said, "you know Tibouchina semidecandra, sometimes listed as Pleroma mecanthrum or Pleroma grandiflora."

"Certainly," Wolfe assented.

I bet he had never heard of it before. Andy went on. "Well, I've got a two-year plant here that I raised from a cutting, less than two feet high, and a branch has sported. The leaves are nearly round, not ovate, foveolate, and the petioles—wait till I show you—it's resting now out of light—"

He had stepped to where a strip of green canvas hung from the whole length of a bench section, covering the space from the waist-high bench to the ground, and, squatting, he lifted the canvas by its free bottom edge and stuck his head and shoulders under the bench. Then he didn't move. For too many seconds he didn't move at all. Then he came back out, bumping his head on the concrete bench, straightened up to his full height, and stood as rigid as if he had been made of concrete himself, facing us, all his color gone and his eyes shut.

When he heard me move his eyes opened, and when he saw me reaching for the canvas he whispered to me, "Don't look. No. Yes, you'd better look."

I lifted the canvas and looked. After I had kept my head and shoulders under the bench about as long as Andy had, I backed out, not bumping my head, and told Wolfe, "It's a dead woman."

"She looks dead," Andy whispered.

"Yeah," I agreed, "she *is* dead. Dead and cooled off."

"Confound it," Wolfe growled.

III

I will make an admission. A private detective is not a sworn officer of the law, like a lawyer, but he operates under a license which imposes a code on him. And in my pocket was the card which put Archie Goodwin under the code. But as I stood there, glancing from Wolfe to Andy Krasicki, what was in the front of my mind was not the next and proper step according to the code, but merely the thought that it was one hell of a note if Nero Wolfe couldn't even take a little drive to Westchester to try to lasso an orchid tender without a corpse butting in to gum the works. I didn't know then that Wolfe's need for an orchid tender was responsible for the corpse being there that day, and that what I took for coincidence was cause and effect.

Andy stayed rigid. Wolfe moved toward the canvas, and I said, "You can't bend over that far."

But he tried to, and, finding I was right, got down on his knees and lifted the canvas. I squatted beside him. There wasn't much light, but enough, considering what met the eye. Whatever had killed her had done things to her face, but it had probably been all right for looks. She had fine light brown hair, and nice hands, and was wearing a blue patterned rayon dress. She lay stretched out on her back, with her eyes open and also her mouth open. There was nothing visible under there with her except an overturned eight-inch flower pot with a plant in it which had a branch broken nearly off. Wolfe withdrew and got erect, and I followed suit. Evidently Andy hadn't moved.

"She's dead," he said, this time out loud.

Wolfe nodded. "And your plant is mutilated. The branch that sported is broken."

"What? Plant?"

"Your Tibouchina."

Andy frowned, shook his head as if to see if it rattled, squatted by the canvas again, and lifted it. His head and shoulders disappeared. I violated the code, and so did Wolfe, by not warning him not to touch things. When he reappeared he had not only touched, he had snitched evidence. In his hand was the broken branch of the Tibouchina. With his middle finger he raked a furrow in the bench soil, put the lower stem of the branch in it, replaced the soil over the stem, and pressed the soil down.

"Did you kill her?" Wolfe snapped at him.

In one way it was a good question and in another way a bad one. It jolted Andy out of his trance, which was okay, but it also made him want to plug Wolfe. He came fast and determined, but the space between the benches was narrow and I was in between. As for plugging me, I had arms too. He stopped close against me, chest to chest, with pressure.

"That won't help you any," Wolfe said bitterly. "You were going to start to work for me tomorrow.

Now what? Can I leave you here with this? No. You'd be in jail before I got home. That question you didn't like, you'll be answering it many times before the day ends."

"Good God." Andy fell back.

"Certainly. You might as well start with me. Did you kill her?"

"No. Good God, no!"

"Who is she?"

"She's—it's Dini. Dini Lauer. Mrs. Pitcairn's nurse. We were going to be married. Yesterday, just yesterday, she said she would marry me. And I'm standing here." Andy raised his hands, with all the fingers spread, and shook them. "I stand here! What am I going to do?"

"Hold it, brother," I told him.

"You're going to come with me," Wolfe said, squeezing past me. "I saw a telephone in the workroom, but we'll talk a little before we use it. Archie, stay here."

"I'll stay here," Andy said. The trance look was gone from his eyes and he was fully conscious again, but his color hadn't returned and there were drops of sweat on his forehead. He repeated it. "I'll stay here."

It took two good minutes to get him to let me have the honor. Finally he shoved off, with Wolfe behind, and after they had left that room I could see them, through the glass partitions, crossing the warm and cool rooms and opening the door to the workroom. They closed it behind them, and I was alone, but of course you're never really alone in a greenhouse. Not only do you have the plants and flowers for company, but also the glass walls give you the whole outdoors. Anyone within seeing distance, in three directions, was really with me, and that led me to my first conclusion: that Dini Lauer, alive or dead, had not been rolled behind that canvas between the hours of seven in the morning and five in the afternoon. The question, alive or dead, made me want a second conclusion, and again I squatted to lift the canvas in search of it. When, some four years previously, the ciphogene tank had been installed in Wolfe's plant rooms to replace cyanogas and Nico-Fume, I had read the literature, which had included a description of what you would look like if you got careless, and a second thorough inspection of Dini's face and throat brought me my second conclusion: she had been alive when she was rolled or pushed under the bench. It was the ciphogene that did it. Since it seemed improbable that she had consciously and obligingly crawled under the bench and lain still, I went on to look and feel for a bump or broken skin, but found neither.

As I got upright again a noise came, knuckles on wood, and then a man's voice, raised to carry through the wood.

"Andy!" It raised some more. "Andy!"

The wood belonged to a large door at the end of the room, the end where the greenhouse was attached to the mansion. The benches stopped some twenty feet short of that end, leaving room for an open space where there was a floor mat flanked by tubs and jars of oversized plants. The pounding came again, louder, and the voice, also louder. I stepped to the door and observed three details: that it opened away from me, presumably into the house, that it was fastened with a heavy brass bolt on my side, and that all its edges, where it met the frame and sill, were sealed with wide bands of tape.

The voice and knuckles were authoritative. No good could come of an attempt to converse through the bolted door, me with the voice of a stranger. If I merely kept still, the result would probably be an invasion at the other end of the greenhouse, via the workroom, and I knew how Wolfe hated to be interrupted when he was having a talk. And I preferred not to let company enter, under the circumstances.

So I slid the bolt back, pushed the door open enough to let myself through, shut it by backing against it, and kept my back there.

The voice demanded, "Who the hell are you?"

It was Joseph G. Pitcairn, and I was in, not a hall or vestibule, but the enormous living room of his house. He was not famous enough to be automatically known, but when we had started, by mail, to try to steal a gardener from him, I had made a few inquiries and, in addition to learning that he was an amateur golfer, a third-generation coupon clipper, and a loafer, I had got a description. The nose alone was enough, with its list to starboard, the result, I had been told, of an accidental back stroke from someone's Number Four iron.

"Where's Andy?" he demanded, without giving me time to tell him who the hell I was.

"My name—" I began.

"Is Miss Lauer in there?" he demanded.

My function, of course, was to gain time for Wolfe. I let him have a refined third-generation grin in exchange for his vulgar glare, and said quietly, "Make it an even dozen and I'll start answering."

"A dozen what?"

"Questions. Or I'll trade you. Have you ever heard of Nero Wolfe?"

"Certainly. What about him? He grows orchids."

"That's one way of putting it. As he says, the point is not who owns them but who grows them. In his case, Theodore Horstmann was in the plant rooms twelve hours a day, sometimes more, but he had to leave because his mother took sick. That was a week ago yesterday. After floundering around, Mr. Wolfe decided to take Andy Krasicki away from you. You must remember that he—"

It wasn't Joseph G. who made me break off. He and I were not alone. Standing back of him were a young man and young woman; off to one side was a woman not so young but still not beyond any reasonable deadline, in a maid's uniform; and at my right was Neil Imbrie, still in his coveralls. It was the young woman who stopped my flow by suddenly advancing and chopping at me.

"Quit stalling and get away from that door. Something's happened and I'm going in there!" She grabbed my sleeve to use force.

The young man called to her without moving, "Watch it, Sibby! It must be Archie Goodwin and he'd just as soon hit a woman as—"

"Be quiet, Donald!" Joseph G. ordered him. "Sybil, may I suggest a little decent restraint?" His cold gray eyes came back to me. "Your name is Archie Goodwin and you work for Nero Wolfe?"

"That's right."

"You say you came to see Krasicki?"

I nodded. "To get him away from you." I rubbed that in hoping to get a nice long argument started, but he didn't bite.

"Does that excuse your bursting into my house and barricading a door?"

"No," I conceded. "Andy invited me into the greenhouse, and I was standing there when I heard you knocking and calling him. He was busy with Mr. Wolfe, and I saw the door was bolted, and I thought it must be you and you certainly had a right to have the door of your own greenhouse opened, so I opened it. As for the barricading, that's where we get to the point. I admit I'm not acting normal. Assuming that the reason is somehow connected with this Miss Lauer, whom I have never met, naturally I would like to know why you asked me if Miss Lauer is in there. Why did you?"

Joseph G. took one long stride, which was all he needed to reach me. "Get away," he said, meaning it.

I shook my head, keeping my grin refined, and opened my mouth to speak just as he reached for me. I had already decided that it wouldn't be tactful to let the cold war get hot, especially since he had Donald and Neil Imbrie in reserve, and that as a last resort I would release some facts, but it didn't get that far. As my muscles tightened in reflex to the touch of his hand, the sound of a car's engine came from outdoors. From where Imbrie stood he had to move only two steps to get a view through a window, and he did so, staring out. Then he turned to his employer.

"State police, Mr. Pitcairn," he said. "Two cars."

Evidently Wolfe's talk with Andy had been short and sour, since he hadn't waited long to do something that he never resorts to if he can help it: calling the cops.

I V

Five hours later, at three o'clock in the afternoon, seated in the one decent chair in the workroom of the greenhouse, Nero Wolfe was making a last frantic despairing try.

"The charge," he urged, "can be anything you choose to make it, short of first degree murder. The bail can be any amount and it will be furnished. The risk will be minimal, and in the end you'll thank me for it, when I've got the facts and you've got to take them."

Three men shook their heads with finality.

One said, "Better give up and get yourself a gardener that's not a killer." That was Ben Dykes, head of the county detectives.

Another said nastily, "If it was me you'd be wanting bail yourself as a material witness." That was Lieutenant Con Noonan of the State Police. He had been a stinker from the start, and it was only after the arrival of the DA, who had good reason to remember the Fashalt case, that Wolfe and I had been accepted as human.

The third said, "No use, Wolfe. Of course any facts you get will be welcome." That was Cleveland Archer, District Attorney of Westchester County. Any common murder he would have left to the help, but not one that a Joseph G. Pitcairn was connected with, no matter how. He went on, "What can the charge be but first degree murder? That doesn't mean the file is closed and I'm ready for trial. Tomorrow's another day, and there are a couple of points that need some attention and they'll get it, but it looks as if he's guilty."

The five of us were alone at last. Wolfe was in the

best chair available, I was perched on a corner of a potting bench, and the other three were standing. The corpse had left long ago in a basket, the army of official scientists had finished and gone, ten thousand questions had been asked and answered by everyone on the premises, the statements had been signed, and Andy Krasicki had departed for White Plains in a back seat, handcuffed to a dick. The law had made a quick clean job of it.

And Wolfe, having had nothing to eat since breakfast but four sandwiches and three cups of coffee, was even more desperate than when he had sent me for the car that dark December morning. Andy had been his, and he had lost him.

The case against him was fair to middling. There was general agreement that he had been jelly for Dini Lauer since he had first sighted her, two months back, when she had arrived to take care of Mrs. Pitcairn, who had tumbled down some steps and hurt her back. That had been testified to even by Gus Treble, the young man in the rainbow shirt, Andy's assistant, who was obviously all for Andy. Gus said that Dini had given Andy the fanciest runaround he had ever seen, which wasn't too bright of Gus if he had his sympathy on straight.

To the question why should Andy want to get rid of Dini the very day she consented to marry him, the answer was, who says she consented? Only Andy. No one else had heard tell of it, and he himself had announced the good news only to Wolfe and me. Then had he fumigated her to death merely because he couldn't have her? That was probably one of the points which the DA thought needed attention. For a judge and jury some Grade A jealousy would have helped. That was a little ticklish, and naturally the

DA wanted a night to sleep on it. Who had been the third point of the jealous triangle? Of those present, Neil Imbrie didn't look the part, Gus Treble didn't act it, and Pitcairn and son were not the sort of people a DA will take a poke at if he can help it. So he couldn't be blamed for wanting to take a look around. Besides, he had asked them all questions, plenty, and to the point, without getting a lead.

Noonan and Dykes had got all their personal timetables early in the game, but when the quickie report on the p.m. had come from White Plains, telling about the morphine, the DA had had another try at them. The laboratory reported that there was morphine present but not enough to kill, and that it could safely be assumed that Dini had died of ciphogene poisoning. The morphine answered one question—how had she been made unconscious enough to stay put under the bench until the ciphogene would take over?—but it raised another one. Was the law going to have to prove that Andy had bought morphine? But that had been a cinch. They had it covered in a matter of minutes. Vera Imbrie, the cook, Neil's wife, whom I had seen in the background in uniform when I invaded the living room, was troubled with facial neuralgia and kept a box of morphine pellets in a cupboard in the kitchen. She hadn't had to use them for nearly a month, and now the box was gone. Andy, along with everyone else, had known about them and where she kept them. It gave the law a good excuse to search the whole house, and a dozen or so spent an hour at it, but found no morphine and no box. Andy's cottage had of course already been frisked, but they had another go at that too.

So the DA checked over their personal timetables with them, but found nothing new. Of course Andy was featured. According to him, at a tête-à-tête in the greenhouse late in the afternoon Dini had at last surrendered and had agreed not only to marry him sometime soon, but also, since he wanted to accept the offer from Nero Wolfe, to quit the Pitcairn job and get one in New York. She had asked him to keep it quiet until she had broken the news to Mrs. Pitcairn. That had been around five o'clock, and he had next seen her some four hours later, a little after nine, when he had been in the greenhouse on his evening round and she had entered through the door that connected with the living room. They had looked at flowers and talked, and then had gone to sit in the workroom and talk some more, and to drink beer, which Dini had brought from the kitchen. At eleven o'clock she had said good night and left via the door to the living room, and that was the last he had seen of her. That's how he told it.

He too had left, by the outside door, and gone to his cottage and written the letter to Wolfe, deciding not to go to bed because, first, he was so excited with so much happiness, and second, he would have to be up at three anyway. He had worked at propagation records and got his things in order ready to pack. At three o'clock he had gone to the greenhouse and had been joined there by Gus Treble, who was to get his last lesson in the routine of preparation for fumigation. After an hour's work, including bolting and taping the door to the living room, and opening the ciphogene master valve in the workroom for eight minutes and closing it again, and locking the outside door and putting up the DOOR TO DEATH sign, Gus had gone home and Andy had returned to the cottage. Again he admitted he had not gone to bed. At seven o'clock he had gone to the greenhouse and opened the vents with outside controls, returned to the cottage, finally felt tired, and slept. At eight-thirty he awoke, ate a quick breakfast and drank coffee, and was ready to leave for the day's work when there was a knock on the door and he opened it to find Nero Wolfe and me.

The timetables of the others, as furnished by them, were less complicated. Gus Treble had spent the evening with a girl at Bedford Hills and stayed late, until it was time to leave for his three o'clock date with Andy at the greenhouse. Neil and Vera Imbrie had gone up to their room a little before ten, listened to the radio for half an hour, and gone to bed and to sleep. Joseph G. Pitcairn had left immediately after dinner for a meeting of the Executive Committee of the Northern Westchester Taxpayers' Association, at somebody's house in North Salem, and had returned shortly before midnight and gone to bed. Donald, after dining with his father and Dini Lauer, had gone to his room to write. Asked what he had written, he said fiction. He hadn't been asked to produce it. Sybil had eaten upstairs with her mother, who was by now able to stand up and even walk around a little but wasn't venturing downstairs for meals. After eating, she had read aloud to her mother for a couple of hours and helped her with going to bed, and had then gone to her own room for the night.

None of them had seen Dini since shortly after dinner. Asked if it wasn't unusual for Dini not to make an evening visit to the patient she was caring for, they all said no, and Sybil explained that she was quite capable of turning down her mother's bed for her. Asked if they knew about Mrs. Imbrie's morphine pellets and where the box was kept, they all said certainly. They all admitted that no known fact excluded the possibility that one of them, sometime between eleven and three, had got Dini to drink a glass of beer with enough morphine in it to put her out, and, after the morphine took, had carried her to the greenhouse and rolled her under the bench, but the implication didn't seem to quicken anyone's pulse except Vera Imbrie's. She was silly enough to assert that she hadn't known Andy was going to fumigate that night, but took it back when reminded that everyone else admitted that the word of warning had been given to all as usual. The cops didn't hold it against her, and I concede that I didn't either.

Nor were there any contradictions about the morning. The house stirred late and breakfast was free-lance. Sybil had had hers upstairs with her mother. They hadn't missed Dini and started looking for her until after nine o'clock, and their inquiries had resulted in the gathering in the living room and Pitcairn's knocking on the door to the greenhouse and yelling for Andy.

It was all perfectly neat. No visible finger pointed anywhere except at Andy.

"Someone's lying," Wolfe insisted doggedly.

The law wanted to know, "Who? What about?"

"How do I know?" He was plenty exasperated. "That's your job! Find out!"

"Find out yourself," Lieutenant Noonan sneered.

Wolfe had put questions, such as, if Andy wanted to kill, why did he pick the one spot and method that would point inevitably to him? Of course their answer was that he had picked that spot and method because he figured that no jury would believe that he had been fool enough to do so, but that was probably another point which the DA thought needed attention. I had to admit, strictly to myself, that none of Wolfe's questions was unanswerable. His main point, the real basis of his argument, was a little special. Other points, he contended, made Andy's guilt doubtful; this one proved his innocence. The law assumed, and so did he, Wolfe, that the flower pot under the bench was overturned when Dini Lauer, drugged but alive, was rolled under. It was inconceivable that Andy Krasicki, not pressed for time, had done that. Firstly, he would have moved the pot out of harm's way; secondly, if in his excitement he had failed to do that and had overturned the pot he would certainly have righted it, and, seeing that the precious branch, the one that had sported, was broken, he would have retrieved it. For such a plant man as Andy Krasicki righting the pot and saving the branch would have been automatic actions, and nothing could have prevented them. He had in fact performed them under even more trying circumstances than those the law assumed, when still stunned from the shock of the discovery of the body.

"Shock hell," Noonan snorted. "When he put it there himself? I've heard tell of your fancies, Wolfe. If this is a sample, I'll take strawberry."

By that time I was no longer in a frame of mind to judge Wolfe's points objectively. What I wanted was to get my thumbs in a proper position behind Noonan's ears and bear down, and, since that wasn't practical, I was ready to break my back helping to spring Andy as a substitute. Incidentally, I had cottoned to Andy, who had handled himself throughout like a two-handed man. He had used one of them, the one not fastened to the dick, to shake hands again with Wolfe just before they led him out to the vehicle.

"All right," he had said, "I'll leave it to you. I don't give a damn about me, not now, but the bastard that did it . . ."

Wolfe had nodded. "Only hours, I hope. You may sleep at my house tonight."

But that was too optimistic. As aforesaid, at three o'clock they were done and ready to go, and Noonan took a parting crack at Wolfe.

"If it was me you'd be wanting bail yourself as a material witness."

I may get a chance to put thumbs on him yet some day.

V

After they had left I remarked to Wolfe, "In addition to everything else, here's a pleasant thought. Not only do you have no Andy, not only do you have to get back home and start watering ten thousand plants, but at a given moment, maybe in a month or maybe sooner, you'll get a subpoena to go to White Plains and sit on the witness stand." I shrugged. "Well, if it's snowy and sleety and icy, we can put on chains and stand a fair chance of getting through."

"Shut up," he growled. "I'm trying to think." His eyes were closed.

I perched on the bench. After some minutes he growled again. "I can't. Confound this chair."

"Yeah. The only one I know of that meets the requirements is fifty miles away. By the way, whose guests are we, now that he who invited us in here has been stuck in the coop?"

I got an answer of a kind, though not from Wolfe. The door to the warm room opened, and Joseph G. was with us. His daughter Sybil was with him. By that time I was well acquainted with his listed nose, and with her darting green eyes and pointed chin.

He stopped in the middle of the room and inquired frostily, "Were you waiting for someone?"

Wolfe opened his eyes halfway and regarded him glumly. "Yes," he said.

"Yes? Who?"

"Anyone. You. Anyone."

"He's eccentric," Sybil explained. "He's being eccentric."

"Be quiet, Sybil," Father ordered her, without removing his eyes from Wolfe. "Before Lieutenant Noonan left he told me he would leave a man at the entrance to my grounds to keep people from entering. He thought we might be annoyed by newspapermen or curious and morbid strangers. But there will be no trouble about leaving. The man has orders not to prevent anyone's departure."

"That's sensible," Wolfe approved. "Mr. Noonan is to be commended." He heaved a deep sigh. "So you're ordering me off the place. That's sensible too, from your standpoint." He didn't move.

Pitcairn was frowning. "It's neither sensible nor not sensible. It's merely appropriate. You had to stay, of course, as long as you were needed—but now you're not needed. Now that this miserable and sordid episode is finished, I must request—"

"No," Wolfe snapped. "No indeed."

"No what?"

"The episode is not finished. I didn't mean Mr. Noonan is to be commended by me, only by you. He was, in fact, an ass to leave the people on your premises free to go as they please, since one of them is a murderer. None of you should be allowed to take a single step unobserved and unrecorded. As for—"

Sybil burst out laughing. The sound was a little startling, and it seemed to startle her as much as it did her audience, for she suddenly clapped her hand to her mouth to choke it off.

"There you are," Wolfe told her, "you're hysterical." His eyes darted back to Pitcairn. "Why is your daughter hysterical?"

"I am not hysterical," she denied scornfully. "Anyone would laugh. It wasn't only melodramatic, it was corny." She shook her head, held high. "I'm disappointed in you, Nero. I thought you were better than that."

I think what finally made him take the plunge was her calling him Nero. Up to then he had been torn. It's true that his telling Andy he hoped it would be only a matter of hours had been a commitment of a sort, and God knows he needed Andy, and the law trampling over him had made bruises, especially Lieutenant Noonan, but up to that point his desire to get back home had kept him from actually making the dive. I knew him well, and I had seen the signs. But this disdainful female stranger calling him Nero was too much, and he took off.

He came up out of the chair and was erect. "I am not comfortable," he told Joseph G. stiffly, "sitting here in your house with you standing. Mr. Krasicki has engaged me to get him cleared and I intend to do it. It would be foolhardy to assume that you would welcome a thorn for the sake of such abstractions as justice or truth, since that would make you a rarity almost unknown, but you have a right to be asked. May I stay here, with Mr. Goodwin, and talk with you and your family and servants, until I am either satisfied that Mr. Krasicki is guilty or am equipped to satisfy others that he isn't?"

Sybil, though still scornful, nodded approvingly. "That's more like it," she declared. "That rolled."

"You may not," Pitcairn said, controlling himself. "If the officers of the law are satisfied, it is no concern of mine that you are not." He put his hand in his side coat pocket. "I've been patient and I'm not going to put up with any more of this. You know where your car is."

His hand left the pocket, and damned if there wasn't a gun in it. It was a Colt .38, old but in good condition.

"Let me see your license," I said sternly.

"Pfui." Wolfe lifted his shoulders a millimeter and let them down. "Very well, sir, then I'll have to manage." He put his hand into his own side pocket, and I thought my God, he's going to shoot it out with him, but when the hand reappeared all it held was a key. "This," he said, "is the key to Mr. Krasicki's cottage, which he gave me so I could enter to collect his belongings—whatever is left of them after the illegal visitations of the police. Mr. Goodwin and I are going there, unaccompanied. When we return to our car we shall await you or your agent to inspect our baggage. Have you any comment?"

"I—" Pitcairn hesitated, frowning, then he said, "No."

"Good." Wolfe turned and went to a table for his coat, hat, and cane. "Come, Archie." He marched.

As we reached the door Sybil's voice came at our backs. "If you find the box of morphine don't tell anybody."

Outdoors I held Wolfe's coat for him and got mine on. The whole day had been dark, but now it was getting darker, though a cold wind was herding the clouds down to the horizon and on over. When we reached the rear of the house I swung left for a detour to the car to get a flashlight, and caught up with Wolfe on the path. No ducking was necessary now, as the twigs had dried. We passed the tennis court and entered the grove of evergreens, where it was already night.

I glanced at my wrist. "Four o'clock," I announced cheerily to Wolfe, who was ahead. "If we were home, and Theodore was still there, or Andy had come, you would be just going up to the plant rooms to poke around."

He didn't even tell me to shut up. He was way beyond that.

It was dark enough in the cottage to need lights, and I turned them on. Wolfe glanced around, spotted a chair nearly big enough, took off his hat and coat, and sat, while I started a tour. The dicks had left it neat. This medium-sized room wasn't bad, though the rugs and furniture had seen better days. To the right was a bedroom and to the left another one, and in the rear was a bathroom and a kitchen.

I took only a superficial look and then returned to Wolfe and told him, "Nothing sticks out. Shall I pack?"

"What for?" he asked forlorn.

"Shall I see if they missed something important?"

He only grunted. Not feeling like sitting and looking at him, I began a retake. A desk and a filing cabinet yielded nothing but horticultural details and some uninteresting personal items, and the rest of the room nothing at all. The bedroom at the left was even blanker. The one at the right was the one Andy had used, and I went over it good, but if it contained anything that could be used to flatten Lieutenant Noonan's nose I failed to find it. The same for the bathroom. And ditto for the kitchen, except that at the rear of a shelf, behind some packages of prunes and cereals, I dug up a little cardboard box. There was no morphine in it, and there was no reason to suppose there ever had been, and I reported its contents to Wolfe merely to get conversation started.

"Keys," I said, jiggling the box, "and one of them is tagged d-u-p period g-r-n-h-s period, which probably means duplicate to the greenhouse. It would come in handy if we want to sneak in some night and swipe that Phalaenopsis."

No comment. I put the keys in my pocket and sat down.

Pretty soon I spoke. "I'd like to make it plain," I said distinctly, "that I don't like the way you're acting. Many times, sitting in the office, you have said to me, 'Archie, go get Whosis and Whosat and bring them here.' Usually, I have delivered. But if you now tell me to drive you home, and, upon arriving, tell me to go get the Pitcairns and Imbries and Gus Treble, which is what I suspect you of, save it. I wouldn't even bother to answer, not after the way you've bitched it up just because a pretty girl called you by your first name."

"She isn't pretty," he growled.

"Nuts. Certainly she's pretty, though I don't like her any better than you do. I just wanted to make sure that you understand what the situation will be if we go home."

He studied me. After a while he nodded, with his lips compressed, as if in final acceptance of an ugly fact.

"There's a phone," he said. "Get Fritz."

"Yeah, I saw it, but what if it's connected with the house?"

"Try it."

I went to the desk and did so, dialing the operator, and, with no audible interference, got her, gave the number, and heard Fritz's voice in my ear. Wolfe got up and came across and took it away from me.

"Fritz? We have been delayed. No, I'm all right. I don't know. The delay is indefinite. No, confound it, he's in jail. I can't tell now but you'll hear from me again well before dinnertime. How are the plants? I see. No, that's all right, that won't hurt them. I see. No no no, not those on the north! Not a one! Certainly I did, but . . ."

I quit listening, not that I was callous, but because my attention was drawn elsewhere. Turning away, for no special reason, a window was in my line of vision, and through it, outdoors near the pane, I saw a branch of a shrub bob up and down and then wiggle to a stop. I am no woodsman, but it didn't seem reasonable that wind could make a leafless branch perform like that, so I turned to face Wolfe again, listened for another minute, and then sauntered across the room and into the kitchen. I switched off the light there, carefully and silently eased the back door open, slipped outside, and pulled the door to.

It was all black, but after I had stood half a minute I could see a little. I slipped my hand inside my vest to my shoulder holster, but brought it out again empty; it was just an automatic check. I saw now that I was standing on a concrete slab only a shallow step above the ground. Stepping off it to the left, I started, slow motion, for the corner of the house. The damn wind was so noisy that my ears weren't much help. Just as I reached the corner a moving object came from nowhere and bumped me. I grabbed for it, but it, instead of grabbing, swung a fist. The fist was hard when it met the side of my neck, and that got me sore. I sidestepped, whirled, and aimed one for the object's kidney, but there wasn't enough light for precision and I missed by a mile, nearly cracking a knuckle on his hip. He came at me with a looping swing that left him as open as a house with a wall gone, I ducked, and he went on by and then turned to try again. When he turned I saw who it was: Andy's assistant, Gus Treble.

I stepped back, keeping a guard up for defense only.

"Lookit," I said, "I'd just as soon go on if you really want to, but why do you want to? It's more fun when I know what it's for."

"You double-crossing sonofabitch," he said, not panting.

"Okay, but it's still vague. Who did I cross? Pitcairn? The daughter? Who?"

"You made him think you were with him and then you helped get him framed."

"Oh. You think we crossed Andy?"

"I know damn well you did."

"Listen, brother." I let my guard down. "You know what you are? You're the answer to a prayer. You're what I wanted for Christmas. You're dead wrong, but you're wonderful. Come in and have a talk with Nero Wolfe."

"I wouldn't talk with that crook."

"You were looking at him through a window. What for?"

"I wanted to see what you were up to."

"That's easy. You should have asked. We were up to absolutely nothing. We were sunk up to our ears. We were phut. We were and are crazy for Andy. We wanted to take him home with us and pamper him, and they wouldn't let us."

"That's a goddam lie."

"Very well. Then you ought to come in and tell Mr.

Wolfe to his face that he's a double-crosser, a crook, and a liar. You don't often get such a chance. Unless you're afraid. What are you afraid of?"

"Nothing," he said, and wheeled and marched to the kitchen door, opened it, and went in. I was right behind.

Wolfe's voice boomed from the other room. "Archie! Where the devil—"

We were with him. He had finished with the phone. He shot a glance at Gus and then at me.

"Where did you get him?"

I waved a hand. "Oh, out there. I've started deliveries."

VI

It took a good ten minutes to convince Gus Treble that we were playing it straight, and though Wolfe used a lot of his very best words and tones, it wasn't words that put it over, it was logic. The major premise was that Wolfe wanted Andy in his plant rooms, quick. The minor was that Andy couldn't be simultaneously in Wolfe's plant rooms and in the coop at White Plains, or in the death house at Sing Sing. Gus didn't have to have the conclusion written out for him, but even so it took ten minutes. The last two were consumed by my recital, verbatim, of the conversation with Joseph G. and Sybil just before leaving the greenhouse.

Gus was seated at the desk, turned to face Wolfe, and I was straddling a straight-backed chair.

"Last July," Gus said, "that Noonan beat up a friend of mine, for nothing."

Wolfe nodded. "There you are. A typical uni-

formed blackguard. I take it, Mr. Treble, that you
share my opinion that Mr. Krasicki didn't kill that
woman. And I heard you tell those men that you
didn't, so I won't pester you about it. But though you
answered freely and fully all questions concerning
yourself, you were manifestly more circumspect regarding others. I understand that. You have a job
here and your words were being recorded. But it
won't do for me. I want to get Mr. Krasicki out of jail,
and I can do so only by furnishing a replacement for
him. If you want to help you can, but not unless you
forget your job, discard prudence, and tell me all you
know about these people. Well, sir?"

Gus was scowling, which made him look old
enough to vote. In the artificial light he looked paler
than he had outdoors in the morning, and his rainbow
shirt looked brighter.

"It's a good job," he muttered, "and I love it."

"Yes," Wolfe agreed sympathetically, "Mr.
Krasicki told me you were competent, intelligent, and
exceptionally talented."

"He did?"

"Yes, sir. He did."

"Goddam it." Gus's scowl got blacker. "What do
you want to know?"

"About these people. First, Miss Lauer. I gathered that you were not yourself attracted by her."

"Me? Not that baby. You heard what I told them.
She was out for a sucker."

"You mean out for money?"

"No, not money. I don't think so. Hell, you know
the kind. She liked to see males react, she got a kick
out of it. She liked to see females react too. Even Neil
Imbrie, old enough to be her father, you should have
seen her giving him the idea when his wife was there.

Not that she was raw; she could put it in a flash and then cover. And what she could do with her voice! Sometimes I myself had to walk off. Anyhow I've got a girl at Bedford Hills."

"Wasn't Mr. Krasicki aware of all this?"

"Andy?" Gus leaned forward. "Listen. That was one of those things. From the first day he glimpsed her and heard her speak, he got drowned. He didn't even float, he just laid there on the bottom. And him no fool, anything but, but it hit him so quick and hard he never got a chance to analyze. Once I undertook to try a couple of words, very careful, and the look he gave me! It was pathetic." Gus shook his head. "I don't know. If I had known he had talked her into marrying him I might have fumigated her myself, just as a favor to him."

"Yes," Wolfe agreed, "that would have been an adequate motive. So much for you. You mentioned Mr. Imbrie. What about him? Assume that Miss Lauer also gave him the idea when his wife was *not* there, that he reacted like a male, as you put it, that developments convinced him that he was in heaven, that she told him last evening of her intention to go away and marry Mr. Krasicki, and that he decided she must die. Are those assumptions permissible?"

"I wouldn't know. They're not mine, they're yours."

"Come come," Wolfe snapped. "I'm not Mr. Noonan, thank God. Prudence will get us nowhere. Has Mr. Imbrie got that in him?"

"He might, sure, if she hooked him deep enough."

"Have you any facts that contradict the assumptions?"

"No."

"Then we'll keep them. You understand, of course,

that there are no alibis. There were four hours for it: from eleven o'clock, when Miss Lauer said good night to Mr. Krasicki and left him, to three o'clock, when you and Mr. Krasicki entered the greenhouse to fumigate. Everyone was in bed, and in separate rooms except for Mr. and Mrs. Imbrie. Their alibi is mutual, but also marital and therefore worthless. His motive we have assumed. Hers is of course implicit in the situation as you describe it, and besides, women do not require motives that are comprehensible by any intellectual process."

"You said it," Gus acquiesced feelingly. "They roll their own."

I wondered what the girl at Bedford Hills had done now. Wolfe went on.

"Let's finish with the women. What about Miss Pitcairn?"

"Well—" Gus opened his mouth wide to give his lips a stretch, touched the upper one with the tip of his tongue, and closed up again. "I guess I don't understand her. I feel as if I hate her, but I don't really know why, so maybe I don't understand her."

"Perhaps I can help?"

"I doubt it. She puts up a hell of a front, but one day last summer I came on her in the grove crying her eyes out. I think it's a complex, only she must have more than one. She had a big row with her father one day on the terrace, when I was working there in the shrubs and they knew it—it was a couple of weeks after Mrs. Pitcairn's accident and he was letting the registered nurse go and sending for a practical nurse which turned out later to be this Dini Lauer—and Miss Pitcairn was raising the roof because she thought she ought to look after her mother herself. She screamed fit to be tied, until the nurse called down from an upstairs window to please be quiet. Another thing, she not only seems to hate men, she says right out that she does. Maybe that's why I feel I hate her, just to balance it up."

Wolfe made a face. "Does she often have hysterics?"

"I wouldn't say often, but of course I'm hardly ever in the house." Gus shook his head. "I guess I don't understand her."

"I doubt if it's worth an effort. Don't try. What I'd like to get from you, if you have it, is not understanding but a fact. I need a scandalous fact about Miss Pitcairn. Have you got one?"

Gus looked bewildered. "You mean about her and Dini?"

"Her and anyone or anything. The worse the better. Is she a kleptomaniac or a drug addict? Does she gamble or seduce other women's husbands or cheat at cards?"

"Not that I know of." Gus took a minute to concentrate. "She fights a lot. Will that help?"

"I doubt it. With what weapons?"

"I don't mean weapons; she just fights—with family, friends, anyone. She always knows best. She fights a lot with her brother. As far as he's concerned, it's a good thing somebody knows best, because God knows he don't."

"Why, does he have complexes too?"

Gus snorted. "He sure has got something. The family says he's sensitive—that's what they tell each other, and their friends, and him. Hell, so am I sensitive, but I don't go around talking it up. He has a mood every hour on the hour, daily including Sundays and holidays. He never does a damn thing, even pick flowers. He's a four-college man—he got booted out of

Yale, then Williams, then Cornell, and then something out in Ohio."

"What for?" Wolfe demanded. "That might help."

"No idea."

"Confound it," Wolfe complained, "have you no curiosity? A good damning fact about the son might be even more useful than one about the daughter. Haven't you got one?"

Gus concentrated again, and when a minute passed without any sign of contact on his face, Wolfe insisted, "Could his expulsion from those colleges have been on account of trouble with women?"

"Him?" Gus snorted again. "If he went to a nudist camp and they lined the men up on one side and the women on the other, he wouldn't know which was which. With clothes on I suppose he can tell. Not that he's dumb, I doubt if he's a bit dumb, but his mind is somewhere else. You asked if he has complexes—"

There was a knock at the door. I went and opened it and took a look, and said, "Come in."

Donald Pitcairn entered.

I had surveyed him before, but now I had more to go on and I checked. He didn't look particularly sensitive, though of course I didn't know which mood he had on. He had about the same weight and volume as me, but it's no flattery to say that he didn't carry them the same. He needed tuning. He had dark deep-set eyes, and his face wouldn't have been bad at all if he had felt better about it.

"Oh, you here, Gus?" he asked, which wasn't too bright.

"Yeah, I'm here," Gus replied, getting that settled.

Donald, blinking in the light, turned to Wolfe. His idea was to make it curt. "We wondered why it took so long to pack Andy's things. That's what you said you wanted to do, but it doesn't look as if you're doing it."

"We were interrupted," Wolfe told him.

"I see you were. Don't you think it would be a good idea to go ahead and pack and get started?"

"I do, yes. We'll get at it shortly. I'm glad you came, Mr. Pitcairn, because it provides an opportunity for a little chat. Of course you are under—"

"I don't feel like chatting," Donald said apologetically, and turned and left.

The door closed behind him and we heard his steps across the porch.

"See?" Gus demanded. "That's him to a T. Papa told him to come and chase you out, and did you hear him?"

"Yes, I heard him. With sensitive people you never know." Wolfe sighed. "We'd better get on, since I want to get back to the house before Mr. Pitcairn decides to come at us himself. What about him? Not what he's like, I've seen him and spoken with him, but the record—what you know of it. I got the impression this afternoon that he does not share his son's confusion about the sexes. He can tell a woman from a man?"

"I'll say he can." Gus laughed shortly. "With his eyes shut. From a mile off."

"You say that as if you could prove it."

Gus had his mouth open to go on, but he shut it. He cocked an eye at Wolfe, tossed me a glance, and regarded Wolfe again.

"Oh," he said. "Now you want me to prove things."

"Not at all. I don't even insist on facts. I'll take surmises—anything you have."

Gus was considering, rubbing the tips of his thumbs with his forefingers and scowling again. Finally he made a brusque gesture. "To hell with it," he decided. "I was sore at you for crossing Andy, and you don't owe him anything, and here look at me. There's other jobs. He choked a girl once."

"Mr. Pitcairn did?"

"Yes."

"Choked her to death?"

"Oh, no, just choked her. Her name's Florence Hefferan. Her folks used to live in a shack over on Greasy Hill, but now they've got a nice house and thirty acres down in the valley. I don't think it was Florence that used the pliers on him, or if she did her old man made her. I know for a fact it took twenty-one thousand dollars to get that thirty acres, and also Florence was by no means broke when she beat it to New York. If it didn't come from Pitcairn, then where? There are two versions about the choking. One is that he was nuts about her and he was jealous because he thought the baby she was going to have wasn't his—that's what Florence told her best friend, who is a friend of mine. The other is that he was sore because he was being forced to deliver some real dough—that came from Florence too, later, after she had gone to New York, I guess because she thought it sounded better. Anyhow I know he choked her enough to leave marks because I saw them."

"Well." Wolfe was looking as pleased as if someone had just presented him with thirty acres of orchids. "When did this happen?"

"About two years ago."

"Do you know where Miss Hefferan is now?"

"Sure, I can get her address in New York."

"Good." Wolfe wiggled a finger. "I said I wouldn't insist on proof, and I won't, but how much of this is fact and how much gossip?"

"No gossip at all. It's straight fact."

"Has any of it ever been published? For instance, in a newspaper reporting a proceeding in a court?"

Gus shook his head. "It wasn't in a court. How would it get in a court when he paid forty or fifty thousand to keep it out?"

"Just so, but I wanted to be sure. Were these facts generally known and discussed in the neighborhood?"

"Well—not known, no." Gus gestured. "Of course there was some talk, but only two or three really knew what happened, and I happened to be one of them because of my friend being Florence's best friend. And I didn't help start any talking. I've never opened my trap about it until now, and I told you only to help Andy, but damned if I see how it's going to."

"I do," Wolfe said emphatically. "Has Mr. Pitcairn been helpful in any other real estate deals?"

"Not that I know of. He must have lost his head that time. But it's more a question of a guy's general approach, and I've seen him performing with house guests here. What I can say for sure is that his son didn't catch it from him. I don't know why—when a man starts turning gray why don't he realize the whistle has blowed and concentrate on something else? Take you, you show some gray. I'll bet you don't dash around crowing and flapping your arms."

I tittered without meaning to. Wolfe gave me a withering glance and then returned to Gus.

"No, Mr. Treble, I don't. But while your general observations are interesting and sound, they won't help me any. I can use only specific items. I need scandal, all I can get. More about Mr. Pitcairn, I hope?"

But apparently Gus had shot his main wad. He had a further collection of details pertaining to Joseph G., and he was now more than willing to turn the bag up and shake it, but it didn't seem to me to advance Pitcairn's promotion to the grade of murder suspect. For one thing, there wasn't even a morsel about him and Dini Lauer, though, as Gus pointed out, he was an outside man and therefore knew little of what went on in the house.

Finally Wolfe waved Pitcairn aside and asked, "What about his wife? I haven't heard her mentioned more than twice all day. What's she like?"

"She's all right," Gus said shortly. "Forget her."

"Why, is she above reproach?"

"She's a nice woman. She's all right."

"Was her accident really an accident?"

"Certainly it was. She was alone, going down the stone steps into the rose garden, and she took a tumble, that was all."

"How much is she hurt?"

"I guess it was pretty bad, but it's getting better now, so she can sit in a chair and walk a little. Andy's been going up to her room every day for orders—only she don't give orders. She discusses things."

Wolfe nodded. "I can see you like her, but even so there's a question. What valid evidence have you that she is incapable of carrying an object weighing a hundred and ten pounds down a flight of stairs and into the greenhouse?"

"Oh, skip it," Gus said scornfully. "Hell, she broke her back!"

"Very well," Wolfe conceded. "But you should consider that whoever drugged Miss Lauer and carried her through the house was under a pressure that demanded superhuman effort. I advise you never to try your hand at detective work. At least you can tell me where Mrs. Pitcairn's room—no." He wiggled a finger. "Is there paper in that desk? And a pencil?"

"Sure."

"Please sketch me a plan of the house—ground plans of both floors. I heard it described this afternoon, but I want to be sure I have it right. Just roughly, but identify all the rooms."

Gus obliged. He got a pad and pencil from a drawer and set to work. The pencil moved fast. In no time he had two sheets torn from the pad and crossed over to hand them to Wolfe, and told him, "I didn't show the back stairs leading up to the room where Mr. and Mrs. Imbrie sleep, but the little passage upstairs goes there too."

Wolfe glanced at the sheets, folded them, and stuck them in his pocket. "Thank you, sir," he said graciously. "You have been—"

What stopped him was the sound of heavy steps on the porch. I got up to go and open the door, not waiting for a knock, but there was no knock. Instead, there was the noise of a key inserted and turned, the door swung open and a pair entered.

It was Lieutenant Noonan and one of the rank and file.

"Who the hell," he demanded, "do you think you are?"

VII

Gus was on his feet. I whirled and stood. Wolfe spoke from his chair.

"Of course, Mr. Noonan, if that was a rhetorical—"

"Can it. I know damn well who you are. You're a Broadway slickie that thinks you can come up to Westchester and tell us the rules. Get going! Come on. Move out."

"I have Mr. Pitcairn's permission—"

"You have like hell. He just phoned me. And you're taking nothing from this cottage. You may have them buffaloed down in New York, and even the DA and the county boys, but I'm different. Do you want to go without help?"

Wolfe put his hands on the arms of his chair, got his bulk lifted, said, "Come, Archie," got his hat and coat and cane, and made for the door. There he turned, said grimly, "I hope to see you again, Mr. Treble," and was saved the awkwardness of reaching for the knob by my being there to open for him. Outside I got the flashlight from my hip pocket, switched it on, and led the way.

As we navigated the path for the fourth time there were seven or eight things I would have liked to say, but I swallowed them. Noonan and his bud were at our heels and, since Wolfe had evidently decided that we were outmatched, there was nothing for me to do but take it. When, after we were beyond the grove of evergreens, I swung the light up for a glance at the tennis court, there was a deep growl from Wolfe behind, so from there on I kept the light on the path.

We crunched across the gravel to where we had left the car. As I opened the rear door for Wolfe to get in, Noonan, right at my elbow, spoke.

"I'm being generous. I could phone the DA and get an okay to take you in as material witnesses, but you see I'm not. Our car's in front. Stop at the entrance until we're behind. We're going to follow until you're out of the county, and we won't need you back here again tonight or any other time. Got it?"

No reply. I banged the door, opened the front one, slid in beside the wheel, and pushed the starter.

"Got it?" he barked.

"Yes," Wolfe said.

They strode off and we rolled forward. When we reached the entrance to the Pitcairn grounds and stopped, the accomplice Noonan had stationed there flashed a light at us but said nothing.

I told Wolfe over my shoulder, "I'll turn right and go north. It's only ten miles to Brewster, and that's in Putnam County. He only said to leave the county, he didn't say which way."

"Turn left and go to New York."

"But—"

"Don't argue."

So when their lights showed behind I rolled on into the highway and turned left. When we had covered a couple of miles Wolfe spoke again.

"Don't try to be witty. No side roads, no sudden changes of pace, and no speeding. It would be foolhardy. That man is an irresponsible maniac and capable of anything."

I had no comment because I had to agree. We were flat on our faces. So I took the best route to Hawthorne Circle and there, with the enemy right behind, swung into the Sawmill River Parkway. The dashboard clock said a quarter to seven. My biggest trouble was that I couldn't see Wolfe's face. If he was holding on and working, fine. If he was merely nervous and tense against the terrific extra hazards of driving after dark, maybe okay. But if he had settled for getting back home and that was all, I should be talking fast and I wanted to. I couldn't tell. I had never realized how much I depended on the sight of his big creased face.

We made the first traffic light in eleven minutes from Hawthorne Circle, which was par. It was green and we sailed through. Four minutes farther on, at the second light, we were stopped by red, and Noonan's car practically bumped our behind. Off again, we climbed the hills over Yonkers, wound down into the valley and the stretch approaching the toll gates, parted with a dime, and in another mile were passing the sign that announces New York City.

I kept to the right and slowed down a little. If he once got inside his house I knew of no tool that could pry him loose again, but we were now only twenty-five minutes away and from where I sat it looked hopeless.

However, I slowed to thirty and spoke. "We've left Westchester, and Noonan is gone. They turned off back there. That's as far as my orders go. Next?"

"Where are we?"

"Riverdale."

"How soon will we get home?"

But there I fooled you. That's what I was sure he would say, but he didn't. What he said was, "How can we get off of this race course?"

"Easy. That's what the steering wheel's for."

"Then leave it and find a telephone."

I never heard anything like it. At the next opening I left the highway, followed the side drive a couple of blocks and turned right, and rolled up a hill and then down. I was a stranger in the Riverdale section, but anybody can find a drugstore anywhere, and soon I pulled up at the curb in front of one.

I asked if he was going in to phone and he said no, I was. I turned in the seat to get a look at him.

"I don't know, Archie," he said, "whether you have ever seen me when my mind was completely dominated by a single purpose."

"Sure I have. I've rarely seen you any other way. The purpose has always been to keep comfortable."

"It isn't now. It is—never mind. A purpose is something to achieve, not talk about. Get Saul if possible. Fred or Orrie would do, but I'd rather have Saul. Tell him to come at once and meet us—where can we meet?"

"Around here?"

"Yes. Between here and White Plains."

"He's to have a car?"

"Yes."

"The Covered Porch near Scarsdale would do."

"Tell him that. Phone Fritz that we are still delayed and ask him how things are. That's all."

I got out, but even at a risk I wanted to have it understood, so I poked my head in and asked, "What about dinner? Fritz will want to know."

"Tell him we won't be there. I've already faced that. My purpose is enough to keep me from going home, but I wouldn't trust it to get me out again if I once got in."

Evidently he knew himself nearly as well as I knew him. I entered the drugstore and found the booth.

I got Fritz first. He thought I was kidding him, and then, when I made it plain that I was serious, he suspected me of concealing a calamity. He simply couldn't believe that Wolfe was a free man and sound of mind and body, and yet wasn't coming home to dinner. It looked for a while as if I would have to go and bring Wolfe to the phone, but I finally convinced him, and then went after Saul.

As Wolfe had said, Fred or Orrie would do, but Saul Panzer was worth ten of them or nearly anyone else, and I had a feeling that we were going to need the best we could get for whatever act Wolfe was preparing to put on to achieve his dominant purpose. So when I learned that Saul wasn't home but was expected sometime, I gave his wife the number and told her I would wait for a call. It was so long before it came that when I went back out to the car I expected Wolfe to make some pointed remarks, but all he did was grunt. The purpose sure was dominant. I told him that from Saul's home in Brooklyn it would take him a good hour and a quarter to drive to the rendezvous, whereas we could make it easy in thirty minutes. Did he have any use for the extra time? No, he said, we would go and wait, so I got the car moving and headed for the parkway.

When, a little before nine o'clock, Saul Panzer joined us at the Covered Porch, we were at a table in a rear corner, as far as we could get from the band. Wolfe had cleaned up two dozen large oysters, tried a plate of clam chowder and swallowed five spoonfuls of it, disposed of a slice of rare roast beef with no vegetables, and was starting to work on a pile of zwieback and a dish of grape jelly. He hadn't made a single crack about the grub.

By the time Wolfe had finished the zwieback and jelly and had coffee Saul had made a good start on a veal cutlet. Wolfe said he would wait until Saul was through, but Saul said no, go ahead, he liked to hear things while he ate. Wolfe proceeded. First he described the past, enough of it to give Saul the picture, and then gave us a detailed outline of the future as he saw it. It took quite a while, for he had to brief us on all foreseeable contingencies. One of them was the possibility that the key tagged "Dup Grnhs" which was in my pocket wouldn't fit. Another prop was the sketch made by Gus Treble of the ground plans of the mansion. Still another prop was a sheet of plain white paper, donated on request by the management of the Covered Porch, on which Wolfe wrote a couple of paragraphs with my fountain pen. That too was for Saul, and he put it in his pocket.

It sounded to me as if the whole conception was absolutely full of fleas, but I let it pass. If Wolfe was man enough to stay away from dinner at his own table, damned if I was going to heckle just because it looked as if we stood a very fine chance of joining Andy in jail before midnight. The only item I pressed him on was the gun play.

"On that," I told him, "I want it A, B, C. When you're in the cell next to mine, on a five-year ticket, I won't have you keep booming at me that I bollixed it up with the gun. Do I shoot at all and if so when?"

"I don't know," he said patiently. "There are too many eventualities. Use your judgment."

"What if someone makes a dash for a phone?"

"Head him off. Stop him. Hit him."

"What if someone starts to scream?"

"Make her stop."

I gave up. I like to have him depend on me, but I only have two hands and I can't be two places at once.

The arrangement was that Saul was to follow us in his car because it would be useful for a preliminary approach. It was after ten when we rolled out of the parking lot of the Covered Porch and turned north.

When I pulled off the road at a wide place, in the enemy country, the dashboard clock said twelve minutes to eleven, and it had started to snow a little. Saul's car had stopped behind us.

I turned off the lights, got out and went back, and told him, "Half a mile on, maybe a little more, at the left. You can't miss the big stone pillars."

He swung his car back into the road and was off. I returned to our car and climbed in, and turned to face the rear because I thought a little cheerful conversation was called for, but Wolfe wouldn't cooperate, and I well knew why. He was holding his breath until he learned whether Saul would bring good news or bad. Would we be able to drive right in and make ourselves at home? Or . . . ?

The news wasn't long in coming, and it was bad. Saul's car came back, turned around, and parked close behind us, and Saul came to us with snowflakes whirling around him and announced, "He's still there."

"What happened?" Wolfe demanded peevishly.

"I turned in at the entrance, snappy, and he flashed a light at me and yelled. I told him I was a newspaperman from New York, and he said then I'd better get back where I belonged quick because it was snowing. I tried a little persuasion to stay in character, but he was in a bad humor. So I backed out."

"Confound it." Wolfe was grim. "I have no rubbers."

VIII

Before we got to the Pitcairn greenhouse Wolfe fell down twice, I fell four times, and Saul once. My better score, a clear majority, was because I was in the lead.

Naturally we couldn't show a light, and while the snow was a help in one way, in another it made it harder, since enough of it had fallen to cover the ground and therefore you couldn't see ups and downs. For walking in the dark without making much noise levelness is a big advantage, and there was none of it around there at all, at least not on the route we took.

It had to be all by guess. We left the road and took to the jungle a good three hundred yards short of the entrance, to give the guy in bad humor a wide miss. Almost right away we were mountain climbing, and I slipped on a stone someone had waxed and went down, grabbing for a tree and missing.

"Look out, a stone," I whispered.

"Shut up," Wolfe hissed.

Just when I had got used to the slope up, the terrain suddenly went haywire and began to wiggle, bobbing up and down. After a stretch of that it went level, but just as it did so the big trees quit and I was stopped by a thicket which I might possibly have pushed through but Wolfe never could, so I had to detour. The thicket forced me around to the rim of a steep decline, though I didn't know it until my feet told me three times. It was at the foot of that decline that we struck the brook. I realized what the dark streak was only when I was on its sloping edge, sliding in, and I leaped like a tiger, barely reaching the far bank and going to my knees as I landed, which I didn't count as a fall. As I got upright I was wondering how in God's name we would get Wolfe across, but then I saw he was already coming, wading it, trying to hold the skirt of his coat up with one hand and poking his cane ahead of him with the other.

I have admitted I'm no woodsman, and I sure proved it that dark night. I suppose I didn't subtract enough for the curves of the driveway. I had it figured that we would emerge into the open about even with the house, on the side where the greenhouse was. But after we had negotiated a few more mountains, and a dozen more twigs had stuck me in the eye, and I had had all my tumbles, and Wolfe had rolled down a cliff to a stop at Saul's feet, and I was wishing the evergreens weren't so damn thick so I could see the lights of the house, I suddenly realized we had hit a path, and after I had turned left on it and gone thirty steps its course seemed familiar. When we reached the edge of the evergreens and saw the house lights there was no question about it: it was the path we knew.

From there on the going was easy and, since the snow was coming thicker, no belly crawling seemed called for as we neared the house. When we reached the spot where the path branched to the left, toward the south of the house, I turned and asked Wolfe, "Okay?"

"Shut up and go on," he growled.

I did so. We reached the greenhouse at its outer end. I took the key from my pocket and inserted it, and it worked like an angel. I carefully pushed the door open, and we entered, and I got the door shut with no noise. So far so good. We were in the workroom. But was it dark!

According to plan, we took off our snow-covered coats and dropped them on the floor, and our hats. I didn't know until later that Wolfe hung onto his cane, probably to use on people who screamed or dashed for a phone. I led the way again, with Wolfe against my back and Saul against his, through into the cool room, but it wasn't cool, it was hot. It was ticklish going down the alley between the benches, and I learned something new: that with all lights out in a glass house on a snowy night the glass is absolutely black.

We made it without displacing any horticulture, and on through the warm room, which was even hotter, into the medium room. When I judged that we were about in the middle of it I went even slower, stopping every couple of feet to feel at the bottom of the bench on my left. Soon I felt the beginning of the canvas, and got hold of Wolfe's hand and guided him to it. He followed me on a little, and then together we pulled the canvas up and Saul crawled under and stretched out where the body of Dini Lauer had been. Unable to see him, I felt him to make sure he was under before I let the canvas fall. Then Wolfe and I moved on to the open space beyond the end of the benches.

By now it was sure enough that there was no one in the dark greenhouse, and whispers would have been perfectly safe, but there was nothing to say. I took my gun from the holster and dropped it in my side pocket, and moved to the door that opened into the living room, with Wolfe beside me. It was a well-fitted door, but there was a tiny thread of light along the bottom. Now our meanest question would be answered: was the door locked on the inside? I heard the sound of voices beyond the thick door, and that helped. With a firm grasp on the knob, I turned it at about the speed of the minute hand on a clock, and when it came to a stop I pushed slow and easy. It wasn't locked.

"Here we go," I muttered to Wolfe, and flung the door open and stepped in.

The first swift glance showed me we were lucky. All three of them were there in the living room—Joseph G., daughter, and son—and that was a real break. Another break was the way their reflexes took the sight of the gun in my hand. One or more might easily have let out a yell, but no, all three were stunned into silence. Sybil was propped against cushions on a divan with a highball glass in her hand. Donald was on a nearby chair, also with a drink. Papa was on his feet, and he was the only one who had moved, whirling to face us as he heard the door open.

"Everybody hold it," I told them quick, "and no one gets hurt."

The noise from Joseph G. sounded like the beginning of an outraged giggle. Sybil put hers in words.

"Don't you dare shoot! You wouldn't dare shoot!"

Wolfe was moving past me, approaching them, but I extended my left arm to stop him. Shooting was the last thing I wanted, by me or anyone else, since a yell might or might not have been heard by the law out at the entrance but a shot almost certainly would. I stepped across to Joseph G., poked the gun against him, rubbed his pockets, and went to Donald and repeated. I would just as soon have given Sybil's blue dinner dress a rub, but it would have been hard to justify it.

"Okay," I told Wolfe.

"This is a criminal act," Pitcairn stated. The words were virile enough, but his voice squeaked.

Wolfe, who had approached him, shook his head. "I don't think so," he said conversationally. "We had a key. I admit that Mr. Goodwin's flourishing a gun complicates matters, but anyway, all I want is a talk with you people. I asked for it this afternoon and was refused. Now I intend to have it."

"You won't get it." Pitcairn's eyes went to his son. "Donald, go to the front door and call the officer."

"I'm still flourishing the gun," I said, doing so. "I can use it either to slap with or shoot with, and if I didn't intend to when necessary I wouldn't have it."

"More corn," Sybil said scornfully. She hadn't moved from her comfortable position against the cushions. "Do you actually expect us to sit here and converse with you at the point of a gun?"

"No," Wolfe told her. "The gun is childish, of course. That was merely a formality. I expect you to converse with me for reasons which it will take a few minutes to explain. May I sit down?"

Father, daughter, and son said "No" simultaneously.

Wolfe went to a wide upholstered number and sat. "I must overrule you," he said, "because this is an emergency. I had to wade your confounded brook." He bent over and unlaced a shoe and pulled it off, did likewise with the other one, took off his socks, pulled his wet trousers up nearly to his knees, and then leaned to the right to get hold of the corner of a small rug.

"I'm afraid I've dripped a little," he apologized, wrapping the rug around his feet and calves.

"Wonderful," Sybil said appreciatively. "You think we won't drive you out into the snow barefooted."

"Then he's wrong," Pitcairn said furiously. His squeak was all gone.

"I'll get him a drink," Donald offered, moving.

"No," I said firmly, also moving. "You'll stay right here." I still had the formality in my right hand.

"I think, Archie," Wolfe told me, "you can put that

thing in your pocket. We'll soon know whether we stay or go." He glanced around at them, ending with Joseph G. "Here are your alternatives. Either we remain here until we are ready to leave, and are allowed a free hand for our inquiry into the murder of Miss Lauer on these premises, or I go, return to my office in New York—"

"No, you don't," Pitcairn contradicted. He remained standing even after his guest was seated. "You go to jail."

Wolfe nodded. "If you insist, certainly. But that will merely postpone my return to my office until I get bail, which won't take long. Once there, I act. I announce that I am convinced of Mr. Krasicki's innocence and that I intend to get him freed by finding and exposing the culprit. There are at least three papers that will consider that newsworthy and will want to help. All the inmates of this house will become legitimate objects of inquiry and public report. Anything in their past that could conceivably have a bearing on their guilt or innocence will be of interest and printable."

"Aha," Sybil said disdainfully, still reclining.

"The devil of it," Wolfe went on, ignoring her, "is that everyone has a past. Take this case. Take the question of Mr. Hefferan's purchase of a home and acres surrounding it, only a few miles from here. I'm sure you remember the name—Hefferan. Where did he get the money? Where did a certain member of his family go to, and why? The newspapers will want all the facts they can get, all the more since their employees are not permitted to enter these grounds. I shall be glad to cooperate, and I have had some experience at investigation."

Joseph G. had advanced a step and then stiffened. Sybil had left the cushions to sit up straight.

"Such facts," Wolfe went on, "would of course never properly get to a jury trying a man for the murder of Miss Lauer, but they would be of valid concern to the unofficial explorers of probabilities, and the public would like to know about them. They would like to know whether Miss Florence Hefferan still feels any discomfort from the severe choking she got, and whether the marks have entirely disappeared from her throat. They would want to see pictures of her in newspapers, the more the better. They would—"

"You filthy fat louse!" Sybil cried.

Wolfe shook his head at her. "Not I, Miss Pitcairn. This is the inexorable miasma of murder."

"By God," Pitcairn said harshly. He was shaking with fury and trying not to. "I wish I had shot you there today. I wish I had."

"But you didn't," Wolfe said curtly, "and here I am. You will have no secrets left, none of you. If Miss Hefferan has run through the money you paid her and needs more, there will be generous bidders for the story of her life in installments. You see the possibilities. There will even be interest in such details as your daughter's incorrigible talent for picking quarrels, and your son's nomadic collegiate career. Did he leave Yale and Williams and Cornell because the curriculum didn't suit him, or because—"

Without the slightest warning Donald abruptly changed moods. After bouncing up to offer to get Wolfe a drink he had returned to his chair and seemed to be put, but now he came out of it fast and made for Wolfe. I had to step some to head him off. He came against me, recoiled, and started a right for the neighborhood of my jaw. The quicker it was settled the better, so instead of trying anything fancy I knocked his fist down with my left, and with my right slammed the gun flat against his kidney good and hard. He wobbled, then bent, and doubled up to sit on the floor. I disregarded him to face the others, not at all sure of their limitations.

"Stop!" a voice came from somewhere. "Stop it!"

Their eyes left the casualty to turn to the voice. A woman had come from behind some drapes at the side of a wide arch at the far end of the room, and was approaching with slow careful steps. Sybil let out a cry and rushed to her. Joseph G. went too. They got to the newcomer and each took an arm, both talking at once, one scolding and the other remonstrating. They wanted to know how she got downstairs. They wanted to turn her around, but nothing doing. She kept coming, them with her, until she was only a step away from her son, who was still sitting on the floor. She looked down at him and then turned to me.

"How much did you hurt him?"

"Not much," I told her. "He'll be a little sore for a day or two."

Donald lifted his face to speak. "I'm all right, Mom. But did you hear what—"

"Yes, I heard everything."

"You come back upstairs," Joseph G. commanded her.

She paid no attention to him. She was no great treat to look at—short and fairly plump, with a plain round face, standing with her shoulders pulled back, probably on account of her injured back—but there was something to her, especially to her voice, which seemed to come from deeper than her throat.

"I've been standing too long," she said.

Sybil started to guide her to the divan, but she said no, she preferred a chair, and let herself be helped to one and to sit, after it had been moved so that she would be facing Wolfe.

Donald, who had managed to get himself back on his feet, went and patted her on the shoulder and told her, "I'm all right, Mom."

She paid no attention to him either. She was gazing straight at Wolfe.

"You're Nero Wolfe," she told him.

"Yes," he acknowledged. "And you're Mrs. Pitcairn?"

"Yes. Of course I've heard of you, Mr. Wolfe, since you are extremely famous. Under different circumstances I would be quite excited about meeting you. I was behind those curtains, listening, and heard all that you said. I quite agree with you, though certainly you know a great deal more about murder investigations than I do. I can see what we have ahead of us, all of us, if a ruthless and thorough inquiry is started, and naturally I'd like to prevent it if I possibly can. I have money of my own, aside from my husband's fortune, and I think we should have someone to protect us from the sort of thing you described, and certainly no one is better qualified than you. I would like to pay you fifty thousand dollars to do that for us. Half would be paid—"

"Belle, I warn you—" Joseph G. blurted, and stopped.

"Well?" she asked him calmly, and when she had waited for him a moment and he was silent, she went on to Wolfe.

"Certainly it would be foolish to pretend that it

wouldn't be well worth it to us. As you say, everyone has a past, and it is our misfortune that this terrible crime in our house has made us, again as you say, legitimate objects of inquiry. Half of the fifty thousand will be paid immediately, and the other half when—well, that can be agreed upon."

This, I thought, is more like it. We now have our pick of going to jail or taking fifty grand.

Wolfe was frowning at her. "But," he objected, "I thought you said that you heard all I said."

"I did."

"Then you missed the point. The only reason I'm here is that I'm convinced that Mr. Krasicki did not kill Miss Lauer, and how the devil can I protect him and you people too? No; I'm sorry, madam; it's true that I came here to blackmail you, but not for money. I've stated my price: permission to remain here, with Mr. Goodwin, and so make my inquiry privately instead of returning to my office and starting the hullabaloo you heard me describe. For as brief a period as possible; I don't want to stay away from home longer than I have to. I shall expect nothing unreasonable of any of you, but I can't very well inquire unless I am to get answers—as I say, within reason."

"A dirty incorruptible blackmailer," Sybil said bitterly.

"You said a brief period," Donald told Wolfe. "Until tomorrow noon."

"No." Wolfe was firm. "I can't set an hour. But I don't want to prolong it any more than you do."

"If necessary," Mrs. Pitcairn persisted, "I think I could make it more than I said. Much more. I can say definitely that it will be double that." She was as stubborn as a woman, and she sure was willing to dig into her capital.

"No, madam. I told Mr. Goodwin this evening that my mind was dominated by a single purpose, and it is. I did not go home to dinner. I fought my way through a snowstorm, at night, over strange and difficult terrain. I entered by force, supported by Mr. Goodwin's gun. Now I'm going to stay until I'm through, or—you know the alternative."

Mrs. Pitcairn looked at her husband and son and daughter. "I tried," she said quietly.

Joseph G. sat down for the first time and fastened his eyes on Wolfe's face.

"Inquire," he said harshly.

"Good." Wolfe heaved a deep sigh. "Please get Mr. and Mrs. Imbrie. I'll need all of you."

IX

For the last several minutes, since it had become evident that we were going to be invited to spend the night, I had had a new worry. The plan was that as soon as possible after we had got the halter on them Wolfe would get them all into the kitchen, to show him where Mrs. Imbrie had kept her box of morphine pills, and it seemed to me that the appearance of Mrs. Pitcairn had turned that from a chore into a real problem. How could he expect a woman with a bum back to get up from a chair and go to the kitchen with him just to point to a spot on a shelf, when three other people were available, all perfectly capable of pointing?

Or rather, five other people, when Mr. and Mrs. Imbrie had come. She was in a kind of dressing gown instead of her uniform, but he had got into his butler's outfit, and I decided I liked him better in his greasy coveralls. They both looked scared and sleepy, and not a bit enthusiastic. As soon as they were with us Wolfe said he wanted to see where Mrs. Imbrie had kept the box of morphine, and that he would like all of them to come along. His tone indicated that he fully expected to be able to tell from the expressions on their faces which one had snitched the morphine to dope Dini Lauer.

The way they responded showed that my psychology needed overhauling and I shouldn't have worried. Guilty or innocent, granted that the guilty one was present, obviously they thought this was a cinch and what a relief it wasn't starting any tougher. There wasn't even any protest about Mrs. Pitcairn exerting herself, except a question from Sybil.

As they started off, Wolfe in his bare feet, he paused to speak to me.

"Archie, will you put my socks near a radiator to dry? You can wring them out in the greenhouse."

So I was left behind. I picked up the socks, and as soon as they were out of the room I darted into the greenhouse leaving the door open, wrung out the socks with one quick twist over the soil of the bench, stooped to lift the canvas, and muttered, "You awake, Saul?"

"Nuts," he hissed.

"Okay, come on. Mrs. Pitcairn is with us. Don't stop to shut the door after you."

I returned to the living room, crossed to the open door by which the others had left, stood with my back to the voices I could hear in the distance, and watched Saul enter, cross to another door at the far end, which led to the reception hall, and disappear. Then I went and hung the socks on the frame of a magazine rack near a radiator grille, and beat it to the kitchen.

They were gathered around an open cupboard door. After exchanging glances with me Wolfe brought that phase of the investigation to a speedy end and suggested a return to the living room. On the way there Sybil insisted that her mother should go back upstairs, but didn't get far. Mrs. Pitcairn was sticking, and I privately approved. Not only did it leave Saul an open field, but it guaranteed him what he needed most—time. Even if they had wanted to adjourn until morning Wolfe could probably have held them, but it was better this way.

"Now," Wolfe said, when he had got settled in the chair of his choice again with the rug around his feet, "look at it like this. If the police were not completely satisfied with Mr. Krasicki they would be here asking you questions, and you wouldn't like it but you couldn't help it. You are compelled to suffer my inquisition for quite a different reason from the one that would operate in the case of the police, but the result is the same. I ask you questions you don't like, and you answer them as you think best. The police always expect a large percentage of the answers to be lies and evasions, and so do I, but that's my lookout. Any fool could solve the most difficult of cases if everyone told the truth. Mr. Imbrie, did you ever hold Miss Lauer in your arms?"

Imbrie, with no hesitation and in a voice unnecessarily loud, said, "Yes!"

"You did? When?"

"Once in this room, because I thought she wanted me to, and she knew my wife was watching us and I didn't. So I thought I would try it."

"That's a lie!" Vera Imbrie said indignantly.

So the first crack out of the box he had one of them calling another a liar.

Neil spoke sternly to his wife. "I'm telling you, Vera, the only thing to do is tell it straight. When the cops left I thought it was all over, but I know about this man and he's tough. We're not going to do any monkeying about murder. How do I know who else saw me? I'm not going to tell him no, I never went near that girl, and then have someone else say they saw me."

"That's the spirit," Sybil said sarcastically. "We'll all confess everything. You lead the way, Neil."

But within three minutes Neil was lying, saying that his wife hadn't minded a bit catching him trying to make a pass at Dini Lauer. He maintained that she had just passed it off as a good joke.

It went on for over two hours, until my wrist-watch said five minutes to three, and I'm not saying it was dull because it was interesting to watch Wolfe bouncing the ball, first against one and then another, and it was equally interesting to see them handling the returns. But though it wasn't dull it certainly didn't seem to me that it was getting us anywhere, particularly when Wolfe was specializing in horticulture. He spent about a third of the time finding out how they felt about plants and flowers, and actually got into an argument with Joseph G. about hairy begonias. It was obvious what he had in mind, but no matter what they said it wasn't worth a damn as evidence, and I suspected him of merely passing the time waiting for Saul, and hoping against hope as the minutes dragged by.

Aside from horticulture he concentrated mainly on the character and characteristics of Dini Lauer. He tried over and over again to get them started on a free-for-all discussion of her, but they refused to oblige, even Neil Imbrie. He couldn't even get a plain unqualified statement that Sybil would have preferred to take care of her mother herself, their position apparently being that if they gave him an inch he'd want a mile. He certainly didn't get the inch.

As I glanced at my watch at five to three Wolfe pronounced my name.

"Archie. Are my socks dry?"

I went and felt them and told him just about, and he asked me to bring them to him. As he was pulling the first one on Mrs. Pitcairn spoke.

"Don't bother with the wet shoes, since you're going to sleep here. Vera, there's a pair of slippers—"

"No, thank you," Wolfe said energetically. He got the other sock on and picked up a shoe. "Thank heaven I get them big enough." He got his toes in, tugged and pushed, finally got the shoe on and tied the lace, and straightened up to rest. In a moment he tackled the second shoe. By the time he got it on the silence was as heavy as if the ceiling had come down to rest on our heads.

Pitcairn undertook to lift it. "It's nearly morning," he rasped. "We're going to bed. This has become a ridiculous farce."

Wolfe sighed from all the exertion. "It has been a farce from the beginning," he declared. He looked around at them. "But I didn't make it a farce, you did. My position is clear, logical, and invulnerable. The circumstances of Miss Lauer's death—the use of Mrs. Imbrie's morphine, the preknowledge of the fumigation, and others—made it unarguable that she was killed by a familiar of these premises. Convinced with good reason, as I was and am, that Mr. Krasicki didn't do it, it followed that one of you did. There we were

and there we are. I had no notion who it was; I forced
my way in here to find out; and I'm going to stay until
I do—or until you expel me and face the alternative I
have described. I am your dangerous and implacable
enemy. I have had you together; now I'll take you one
by one; and I'll start with Mrs. Pitcairn. It will soon
be dawn. Do you want to take a nap first, madam?"

Mrs. Pitcairn was actually trying to smile. "I'm
afraid," she said in a firm full voice, "that I made a
mistake when I offered to pay you to protect us from
publicity. I'm afraid it made a bad impression on you.
If you misunderstood—*who is that?*"

It was Saul Panzer, entering from behind the
drapes where she had previously concealed herself for
eavesdropping. He was right on the dot, since the arrangement had been for him to walk on at three
o'clock unless he got a signal.

Most of us could get our eyes on him without turning, but Wolfe, in his chair with a high wide back, had
to lean over and screw his head around. While he was
doing that Donald was rising to his feet, and Joseph
G. and Imbrie were both moving. I moved faster.
When I had passed them I whirled and snapped,
"Take it easy. He came with us and he don't bite."

They started ejaculating and demanding. Wolfe ignored them and asked Saul, "Did you find anything?"

"Yes, sir."

"Useful?"

"I think so, yes, sir." Saul extended a hand with a
piece of folded paper in it.

Wolfe took it and commanded me, "Archie, your
gun."

I already had it out. It wasn't desirable to have
them anywhere near Wolfe while he examined Saul's

find. I poked the barrel against Joseph G. and told him, "More formality. Back up."

He was still ejaculating but he went back, and the others with him, and I turned sideways enough to have all in view. Wolfe had unfolded the sheet of paper and was reading it. Saul was at his right hand, and he too was displaying a gun.

Wolfe looked up. "I should explain," he said, "how this happened. This is Mr. Saul Panzer, who works for me. When you went to the kitchen with me he entered from the greenhouse, went upstairs, and began to search. I was not satisfied that the police had been sufficiently thorough." He fluttered the paper. "This proves me right. Where did you find it, Saul?"

"I found it," Saul said distinctly, "under the mattress on the bed in the room of Mr. and Mrs. Imbrie."

Vera and Neil both made noises, and Neil came forward to where my arm stopped him.

"Take it easy," I advised him. "He didn't say who put it there, he just said where he found it."

"What is it?" Mrs. Pitcairn inquired, her voice not quite as firm.

"I'll read it," Wolfe told her. "As you see, it's a sheet of paper. The writing is in ink, and I would judge the hand to be feminine. It is dated December sixth, yesterday—no, since it's past midnight, the day before yesterday. It says:

"Dear Mr. Pitcairn:
    "I suppose now I will never call you Joe, as you wanted me to. I am quite willing to put my request in writing, and I only hope you will put your answer in writing too. As I told you, I think your gift to me should be twenty thousand dollars. You have been so very sweet, but I have been sweet too, and I really think I deserve that much.

"Since I have decided to leave here and get married I don't think you should expect me to wait more than a day or two for the gift. I'll expect you in my room tonight at the usual time, and I hope you'll agree how reasonable I am."

Wolfe looked up. "It's signed 'Dini,'" he stated. "Of course it can be authenti—"

"I never saw it!" Vera Imbrie cried. "I never—"

But her lines got stolen. For my part, I didn't even give her a glance. Their faces had all been something to see while Wolfe had read, as might have been expected, but by the time he had reached the third sentence it was plain that Donald was in for something special in the way of moods. First his face froze, then it came loose and his mouth opened, and then the blood rushed up and it was purple. He was a quick-change artist if I ever saw one, and, as I say, I had no glance to spare for Vera Imbrie when she cried out. Then Donald took over.

"So that's why you wouldn't let me marry her!" he screamed, and jumped at his father.

I had the gun, sure, but that was for us, not for them if and when their ranks broke. The women were helpless, and Neil Imbrie would have had to be bigger and faster than he was to stop that cyclone.

Donald toppled his father to his knees more by bodily impact than by his swinging fists, kicked him down the rest of the way, and bent over him screaming, "You thought I was no man! But I was with her! I loved her! For the first time—I loved her! And you wouldn't let me and she was going away and now I know! By God, if I could kill her I can kill you too! I can! I can!"

It looked as if he might try to prove it, so I went and grabbed him, and Saul came to help.

"Oh, my son," Mrs. Pitcairn moaned.

Wolfe looked at her and growled, "Mr. Krasicki is a woman's son too, madam." I didn't think he had it in him.

X

At six o'clock the next afternoon but one I was at my desk in the office, catching up on neglected details, when I heard the sound of Wolfe's elevator descending from the plant rooms, and a moment later he entered, got himself comfortable in his chair back of his desk, rang for beer, leaned back, and sighed with deep satisfaction.

"How's Andy making out?" I asked.

"Considering the blow he got, marvelously."

I put papers in a drawer and swiveled to face him.

"I was just thinking," I said, not offensively, "that if it hadn't been for you Dini Lauer might still be alive and giving males ideas. Ben Dykes told me an hour ago on the phone that Donald has admitted, along with other things, that her telling him she was leaving and going to get married was what put him into a mood to murder. If you hadn't offered Andy a job he wanted to take he might not have got keyed up enough to talk her into marrying him—or anyhow saying she would. So in a way you might say you killed her."

"*You* might," Wolfe conceded, taking the cap from one of the bottles of beer Fritz had brought.

"By the way," I went on, "Dykes said that ape Noonan is still trying to get the DA to charge you for destroying evidence. Burning that letter you wrote to Pitcairn, signing Dini's name."

"Bah." He was pouring and watching the foam. "It wasn't evidence. No one ever saw what was on it. It could have been blank. I merely read it to them—ostensibly."

"Yeah, I know. Anyhow the DA is in no position to charge you with anything, let alone destroying evidence. Not only has Donald told it and signed it, how she was his first and only romance, how his parents threatened to cross him off the list if he married her, how he begged her not to marry Andy and she laughed at him, how he got her to split a bottle of midnight beer with him and put morphine in hers, and even how he lugged her into the greenhouse to make it nice for Andy—not only that, but Vera Imbrie has contributed details of some contacts between Donald and Dini which she saw."

Wolfe put down the empty glass and got out his handkerchief to wipe his lips. "That of course will help," he said complacently.

I grunted. "Help is no word for it. Would it do any good to ask you exactly what the hell you would have done if they had all simply sneered when you read that letter?"

"Not much." He poured more beer. "I knew one of them was toeing a thin and precarious line, and probably more than one. I thought a good hard jolt would totter him or her, no matter who it was, and possibly others. That was why I had Saul find it in the Imbries' room; they had to be jolted too. If all of them had simply sneered, it would at least have eliminated Mr. Pitcairn and his son, and I would have proceeded from there. That would have been a measurable advance, since up to that point a finger pointed nowhere and I had eliminated no one but Andy, who—"

He stopped abruptly, pushed his chair back, arose, muttered, "Good heavens, I forgot to tell Andy about those Miltonia seedlings," and marched out.

I got up and went to the kitchen to chin with Fritz.

The World of
Rex Stout

Now, for the first time ever, enjoy a peek into the life of Nero Wolfe's creator, Rex Stout, courtesy of the Stout Estate. Pulled from Rex Stout's own archives, here are rarely seen, never-before-published memorabilia. Each title in "The Rex Stout Library" will offer an exclusive look into the life of the man who gave Nero Wolfe life.

Three Doors to Death

Rex Stout worked and corresponded with many of the top American writers of the twentieth century; among them, Pulitzer Prize-winnning poet Carl Sandburg. A 1958 note from Sandburg to Stout is reproduced here.

CONNEMARA FARM
FLAT ROCK, N. C.
June 30, 1958

Dear Rex Stout:

When a fellow like you will take the time to write
that kind of a January 10 letter to me, I feel be-
holden somehow. There is a lurking affection un-
deniably ther e in some of the sentences and to
this I cannot be insensitive. We must have a tall
glass of beer over this sometime in an old fashioned
pla ce where they have sawdust on the floor....I enjoy the fe llowship of craftsmanship that goes with
membership in the Author's Guild. Looking back at
the last sentence I notice I have three ships afloat....
Anyhow your letter haunts me a little and one of
these days I hope to get to a piece for the Authors
Guild Bulletin.

Your w ell-willer

Carl Sandburg